Coming T

This is for Norma and David Z.

But pleasures are like poppies spread –
You seize the flow'r, its bloom is shed;
Or like the snow falls in the river –
A moment white, then melts for ever.

Robert Burns (1759–1796)

THE SWINGERS 4

Coming Through the Rye

Nick Clarke

POCKET BOOKS

New York   London   Toronto   Sydney   Tokyo   Singapore

First published in Great Britain by Pocket Books, 1993
A division of Simon & Schuster Ltd
A Paramount Communications Company

Simon & Schuster Ltd
West Garden Place
Kendal Street
London W2 2AQ

Simon & Schuster of Australia Pty Ltd
Sydney

A CIP catalogue record for this book is
available from the British Library
ISBN 0-671-71769-3

Typeset by Keyboard Services, Luton
Printed and bound in Great Britain by
HarperCollins Manufacturing, Glasgow

❀ ONE ❀

Roamin' In The Gloamin'

Ivor Belling eased slowly into consciousness. He turned his head and buried his face in a shock of golden hair, breathing in its warm scent. Some fine strands of hair tickled his nose and he opened his eyes and looked fondly at the owner of the silky blonde tresses who was sleeping beside him. In the bright morning light he could see the tawny glow of her skin and the soft, full curves of her naked body. The luxurious hotel room was warm and they had generated enough heat from their love-making just over an hour before to sleep on top of the plump, patterned duvet.

He looked at his watch and sighed. As he leaned forward and kissed her lips, the girl woke instantly.

'Time to get up, Chrissie,' said Ivor regretfully as he heaved himself up into a sitting position. 'The audition's not beginning till ten o'clock but I promised to meet my photographer, Brian Lipman, at twenty past nine downstairs in the Macauley suite. We've an awful lot of work to plough through before lunch.'

In reply Chrissie swung over her arm to let her elbow rest on his abdomen whilst she gently stroked Ivor's nipples with her fingers. 'I wouldn't bank on Brian being there sharp at nine twenty. Paula's a passionate lassie and she'll expect him to make love to her before breakfast.'

'Well, that's not uncommon! It won't make him late!'

'That will depend,' she said with a saucy smile.

'Depend on what?' he asked and Chrissie ran her fingers smartly down from Ivor's chest to slide round his flaccid cock. 'Depends how long it takes Paula to get your photographer's equipment into full working order,' she murmured sexily. Her fingers tightened their grip around his stirring member.

'M'mm, I'm glad to see that you've still got some lead in your pencil,' Chrissie added with satisfaction. Still holding tight on Ivor's fast-stiffening prick, she leaned over and pressed her soft lips against his cheek.

Reluctantly, Ivor pulled back from the embrace and tried to compose his thoughts. It was Tuesday May 12th, 1965 and he was here in Glasgow with Brian Lipman on behalf of his company, Cable Publicity. The idea was to work his butt off for International Pet Products, one of the agency's most important clients. The trip had begun in fine style last night with a chance meeting with Chrissie and Paula in the hotel bar. It had led to a pairing off into the men's bedrooms, but he could not afford to foul up the arrangements for the publicity launch of Four Seasons Dog Food.

'Don't excite me, darling,' he begged her. But his voice was already thick and unsteady as the luscious girl slicked her fist up and down his swollen shaft. 'Look, we really don't have time and I don't want to start something I can't finish. It's almost a quarter past eight and –'

He stopped short. A fervent groan escaped from his lips as Chrissie jammed down his foreskin and then swooped down to plant a long wet kiss on the bared helmet of his throbbing tool.

2

'That's not fair,' said Ivor plaintively as she took the smooth knob between her lips and sucked hard, taking at least a third of his rigid rod into her mouth whilst her hands played with·his dangling balls. He could hear the sound of her tongue slurping around his pulsating pole and he closed his eyes as Chrissie continued to lick his cock, drawing her tongue along the sensitive underside. He clutched at her hair and shuddered violently as the girl circled her tongue round the fleshy purple knob so sensuously that any remaining thoughts about getting up and starting work fled from Ivor's mind.

When he opened his eyes he saw that Chrissie was now fingering herself as she sucked happily on his sinewy cock, rubbing her fingertips along the edges of her pouting pussy lips and sliding a finger between them. But from his hoarse panting, she realised that watching her masturbate aroused Ivor to boiling point. So she moved her hands from her moist honeypot to his quivering cock, which she held lightly as she crammed all but the last inch or so into her mouth.

He moved his hips backwards and forwards as Chrissie kept her sweet lips taut on his length, kissing, sucking, licking and lapping. She felt his shaft tremble and he pumped a fierce fountain of sticky white spunk into her mouth. She swallowed his jism as she furiously rubbed his twitching prick to coax out the last drains of his libation.

'You naughty girl,' gasped Ivor as he inhaled deep gulps of air whilst he recovered. 'I'm sorry I came so quickly but you're the sexiest fellatrix who has ever sucked my cock.'

Chrissie looked at him with a suspicious expression. 'Fellatrix? What's that when it's at home?'

'Oh, it's a compliment, I assure you,' he explained,

running his hand through her silky blonde hair. 'Fellatio is the posh name for oral sex and a girl who performs it is known as a fellatrix.'

'Well, that's as maybe, but on Sauchiehall Street we simply call it good old-fashioned cocksucking.' The stunning girl spoke with a touch of asperity as she moved herself up to rest her head on Ivor's shoulder.

He chuckled and kissed her gently on the mouth. 'That's a much simpler and straightforward way of speaking,' said Ivor sincerely as he slid away to pad across to the bathroom.

'I really do have to get up, Chrissie,' he called out and as he turned on the bath-taps he suddenly remembered Chrissie had told him that she and Paula worked on the delicatessen counter at Websters, a large new super-market only a quarter of a mile away from the hotel. 'I would have thought that you and Paula must also start to think about making a move. After all, don't you have to be at work by nine o'clock?'

'No, we're both on the eleven to seven shift today,' she replied and Ivor frowned slightly as he mulled over this information. He really did have to go over the day's arrangements with Brian Lipman before the arrival of Eddie Taylor, the Scottish area manager of International Pet Products, and Jimmy Campbell of the Dolly Birds Model Agency.

Jimmy Campbell had been asked to supply two attractive girls who would add some glamour at the mid-day press conference and give Brian Lipman the chance to take some photographs for the trade press. Then the idea was to take the girls round to a couple of major suburban shopping centres in their colourful costumes, holding the lead of a friendly black labrador in one hand and in the other clutching coupons for half-price tins of Four

4

Seasons to any other people with dogs on a leash – anyone, for that matter, who appeared interested enough.

So Ivor's first task was to select two out of the five girls who Jimmy Campbell would bring round to the hotel. This was now Cable Publicity's standard practice since a model chosen by a Midlands agency to show off the Sandy Aspis range of swimsuits at a fashion show in Birmingham turned out to be so over-fond of gin and tonics that she had insisted on offering a close-up inspection of her bare backside to a straight-laced buyer from a leading chain of retail stores.

After that, he had to check the final details of the promotion with Brian Lipman and then he had to ensure that Eddie Taylor, the International Pet Products' manager, was fully briefed on the promotion. It was of vital importance that the client's representative was impressed with their performance. The IPP work accounted for fifteen per cent of Cable Publicity's income and Ivor's chairman, Martin Reece, spent a great deal of time fighting off challenges from rival public relations agencies who were constantly trying to wrest the prestige account from Cable's care.

And as if this were not enough, Ivor had to attend to the needs of the journalists at the press conference – and also be on hand to help Iain Taylor with the small group of top buyers from the grocery trade who had also been invited to the launch.

There must be an easier way of making a living, he said to himself as he turned off the bath-taps and stepped into the bath. He soaped himself all over and then lay back and soaked his body in the lovely warm water. A few moments later Chrissie wandered in and scrunched up her hair inside a shower-cap. She looked mischievously at Ivor and then came over to him and impudently lifted up his limp penis out of the water. She took the bar of soap out of his hand and smoothed it over his cock, retracting the foreskin to wash his member thoroughly.

'A shower's far more hygienic than a bath,' she remarked as she gave the soap back to Ivor and let his shaft slide back into the water. 'What's the point of cleaning yourself up and then lying back in your own dirt?'

Ivor pondered over her question and finally answered: 'You may well have something there. I'll remember that point if we ever get an account for a shower manu-facturer.'

'Well, it's funny you should say that, Ivor. Because Mike, my brother-in-law, is the Northern Area sales manager of Jetstream Showers! To be truthful, it was Mike who pointed out all the advantages of a shower, it's more etcetera, etcetera.' She picked up his cock again and noted with satisfaction how it started to swell and throb in her hand.

'Jetstream's a Scottish company, you know, and Mike works from their showrooms in Edinburgh,' continued Chrissie as she stroked his stiffened shaft. 'I saw him last week and, come to think of it, he told me that their managing director was planning a trip to London shortly to see if it might be worthwhile for Jetstream to appoint a London PR agency to market their new range next year.'

'Really?' said Ivor with genuine interest. Far-fetched as it might be, introductions to new clients often came in the most extraordinary ways. His boss, Martin Reece, had gained the account for Lloyds of London boxer shorts after being stuck in a lift at the Hilton hotel for twenty-five minutes with the firm's founder. His colleague, Tony Hammond, had scooped up some prestigious work for the

Rubin Foundation, a charitable organisation which offered help to unmarried mothers and their children, after he discovered that his girl friend's uncle was an honorary executive trustee of the Foundation.

'I'd like to meet your brother-in-law whilst I'm up in Scotland, Chrissie,' Ivor added. He stood up and pulled out the plug whilst Chrissie kept a tight hold of his cock. 'Perhaps he could introduce me to the managing director and I could show him what Cable has to offer.'

'No problem, Ivor, so long as you promise to show me what your cock can offer this evening,' she said, holding his organ between the palms of her hands and rolling it to and fro.

'Oh, you have my word on it,' he said instantly, removing her hands from his tingling tool whilst he clambered out of the bath. 'We'll fuck ourselves silly tonight so don't let's spoil our appetite now. Look, I have to rush, I really do, so have your shower and get dressed, there's a good girl, and as you're in no hurry, you can either have breakfast up here by yourself or downstairs with me and Brian whilst we go over our business.'

'I'll join you later, but if Paula puts in an appearance before me, tell her to hang on, I won't be too long.'

'Fine, I'll see you later,' said Ivor, wrapping himself in a bath towel and drying his face. He peered round the room to see where he had left his electric razor.

Fifteen minutes later he was downstairs in the restaurant ordering his breakfast. Very shortly afterwards Brian Lipman pulled up a chair and joined him.

'Well done, Brian, you're dead on time,' said Ivor approvingly to the photographer. 'I knew you wouldn't be late though Chrissie didn't think you'd make it because she said that Paula was very keen on rumpy-pumpy first thing in the morning.'

'You can say that again,' said his colleague with some feeling. 'I've heard how Scots girls like their oats but Paula's insatiable. She woke me up at half past five, half past six *and* half past seven. Every hour on the hour, like trains to Brighton from Victoria! I've left her up in the room and she'll be down in about half an hour. I'm supposed to see her again tonight but, frankly, I don't know whether I'm up to it.'

Ivor gave a little chuckle as he scanned the menu. 'I'm sure you'll have recovered by this evening! Actually, I'd be obliged if you don't let her down. She's Chrissie's best friend and I want to keep on the right side of Chrissie.' Ivor explained how she might be able to help pick up some new business once the Four Seasons launch was over.

'Sounds good, and you don't have to worry! I shouldn't really grumble about Paula. She's a marvellous screw. She's only been on the pill for a few months so she's exceptionally lively, that's all, as she's having such a good time now she doesn't have to worry about being in the pudding club.' Brian turned to the waiter who was now hovering by the table and chose orange juice, bran flakes, kippers, toast and tea for his breakfast.

'I'll have the same, please,' said Ivor and when the waiter turned away he added: 'No forbidden fruit, Brian? I would have put folding money on your ordering bacon and eggs.'

'If it weren't for Katie, I would have done,' said Brian with a heavy sigh. 'But she made me promise that I wouldn't eat anything that wasn't kosher whilst I was away.'

'Katie's your new lady then?' said Ivor. When the photographer gave a confirming nod, he grinned and went on: 'Ah, a nice Jewish girl, Brian? Your old Mum and Dad will be thrilled.'

'Here, steady on,' protested Brian heatedly. 'Katie and I are just very good friends, so don't start making with the wedding bells yet, if you don't mind.'

Ivor held up his hands in surrender but he couldn't resist teasing his friend a little more. 'She's a religious girl, though, Brian, I can see you'll be going to synagogue every week instead of the Spurs.'

'A lot of people do both,' snorted Brian. He rapidly changed the subject by picking up the newspaper. 'Here, Ivor, C. S. Forester died, you know, the man who wrote the Captain Hornblower books. I used to read and re-read them when I was at school. Did you ever read them when you were a kid?'

'Oh sure, my friends and I all loved all those stories about naval battles against the French during the Napoleonic Wars. Forester must have been a great sailor himself.'

'You'd think so, wouldn't you, but this obituary notice says that in fact Forester never sailed and picked up all his information from an old Admiralty manual which he bought in a second-hand bookshop. Well, that shows that you can't judge a book by its covers, doesn't it?'

'Okay, I get the message,' said Ivor as the waiter came up and placed two large glasses of fresh orange juice on the table. 'In other words, just because you won't be eating any bacon at breakfast, this doesn't mean that you and Katie are going to march up the aisle.'

The photographer smiled and raised his glass. 'You've got it in one, *boychick*. It so happens that I *am* smitten by Katie but just at the moment I still want to fuck every pretty girl that comes into the studio. Until that feeling goes, I'm staying single, because I really don't believe that married men should fool around.'

'Then you'll be a bachelor all your life,' Ivor commented promptly. 'You'll *always* want to fuck girls like Elizabeth and Penny.'

'Elizabeth and Penny? Oh, you mean the two girls we met on the train coming up here. Yes, I suppose part of me always will, but I think the time will come when I'll just think how sexy they are and leave it at that. When *that* happens, I'll ask Katie or whoever I'm with at the time if they want to get hitched.'

Ivor smiled and said: 'Right, I'll take your wise words to heart if I ever find myself in that situation. Meanwhile, let's go through the itinerary and make sure we've covered all the bases.

'Eddie Taylor will be here in about a quarter of an hour. Whilst I'm choosing the girls from the Dolly Bird Agency, you could use the time by taking some photographs of Eddie. Take one or two in colour which we could frame and send to him with our compliments.'

'No sweat, Ivor, and I'll send a couple of photos to old what's his name, IPP's in-house PRO at the same time. He'll be grateful for a shot of Iain if he rises higher in the company. Incidentally, why isn't he coming to the launch?'

'You're talking about Ronnie Harrison, and he's not here because he gave in his notice last week. He's got a better job with Vauxhall Motors. They've given his job to Ronnie's assistant, Sally Reynolds. I don't think you've met her, have you?'

'No, not yet, but why isn't she here then?' asked Brian.

'Because there's a presentation of a £5,000 cheque to the winner of the Choice Cuts' Most Lovable Crossbreed competition in London today,' explained Ivor patiently.

'Blimey, what will the dog do with all that money?'

'Pee on the cheque, I dare say. Believe it or not, it's not the dog but the mutt's owner who collects the cash. Anyhow, Sally, will have her hands full so we're on our own. It gives us a chance to show what we can do, though you know how careful we have to be with this account. We've had it for three years and half the agencies in town are still trying to grab it from us. So everything has to run like clockwork.'

'Don't worry, it'll all be well. Even the weather's on our side. The sun's shining and I heard on the radio that they don't expect any rain till tomorrow. So the girls will be able to start their stuff outside and with a bit of luck we might even get a few seconds on the telly if Mrs Rokeby turns up trumps.'

'Oh yes, I'd quite forgotten about Mrs Rokeby. She's the top golden labrador breeder who is going to swear that her dogs prefer Four Seasons to any other dog food,' mused Ivor thoughtfully. 'She'll be here at eleven with Charlie, the dog who she promises will always eat the bowl of Four Seasons first even when four other bowls of other tinned dog food are also on offer.'

Brian Lipman let out a short laugh. 'Probably because the hound knows he'll get a swift kick in the balls if he doesn't make tracks straightaway for the right bowl,' he commented cynically.

'That's Charlie's problem, not ours,' grunted Ivor. 'Mrs Rokeby is kindly bringing some dog bowls and Eddie Taylor's supplying tins of all the other brands as well as our own. We'll then invite one of the journalists to choose which tins we open in the Four Seasons Challenge and let's just pray that Charlie does the business for us.'

'Stop worrying,' repeated Brian, jerking his head towards the restaurant entrance. 'Mark my words, any day that starts with a good gobble never turns out bad.

Anyhow, start with the smiles, I think that your friend from IPP has arrived.'

Ivor looked up to see a slightly built, good-looking young man in his late twenties holding a smart leather briefcase being directed to their table by a waiter. 'Yup, that must be him,' he muttered as he rose from his chair and extended a hand. 'Eddie Taylor? Good to see you! I'm Ivor Belling and this gentleman – using the word in its loosest sense – is Brian Lipman, our photographer.'

'You should hear what he says about people he doesn't get on with,' said Brian as he also rose and shook hands with the newcomer.

Eddie Taylor chuckled as he pulled over a chair from an adjoining table and sat down with them. 'Good to meet you both. You had a good journey up from London?'

'Yes, it was fine*. The hotel's very comfortable so we've been having a nice break away from the office,' said Ivor, calling a waiter over to them. 'Have you had breakfast, Eddie?'

'I have, thank you, but a cup of tea would be welcome,' he replied. He unlocked the straps of his briefcase and took out a notebook and pen. 'Now, Ivor, before kick-off, there's something important I want to say to you.'

He leaned forward over the table and Ivor and Brian followed suit as he lowered his voice and continued: 'This promotion is vital as far as I'm concerned. You know Jeff Mountjoy, Ivor?'

'Of course I do, Jeff's been my contact at IPP ever since I began work on the account. He rang me only the other day to wish us luck and to say that he was sorry he couldn't make it up to Glasgow himself.'

'And did he tell you why he's not coming? Well,

---

* see *The Swingers 3 – Public Affairs*, Pocket Books.

between ourselves, Jeff's given in his notice and he'll leave IPP in four weeks' time. His wife comes from a small town somewhere in Devon and she's never settled in Manchester so he's found himself another job down in Southampton with Tagholm Sportswear.'

'That's the second defection in a month. Your press officer leaves next week,' said Ivor with a slight frown. Like all agency directors, he disliked management changes in his clients' firms, unless Cable Publicity found it hard to work with the incumbent executive. Often the new men wanted to sweep away all the relics of the previous administration and this often meant changing their suppliers.

'I know, and Sally Reynolds is taking over from him. She's a good girl and once she gets her feet under the desk she'll do a better job than Ronnie Harrison. He was too busy getting his leg over to get much work done.'

Brian Lipman nodded his agreement at this last remark. 'You're absolutely right there, Eddie,' he agreed. 'You must have worried about wearing your kilt at the Christmas Party as Ronnie would try to screw anything in a skirt.'

Eddie smiled and went on: 'So I would have been if I had one but I've never worn the kilt as actually I was born in Walthamstow! Anyway, I'm sure you're more concerned about Jeff retiring from the fray. The point is, there'll soon be a vacancy for a deputy marketing director at IPP's headquarters in Manchester and if Four Seasons takes off in Scotland, my hat will be in the ring. I've not been given any promises but I've been told off the record that the big boys believe in Four Seasons and if the test market sales go well up here, I'll be able to walk into Jeff's job.

'And if I do, I won't forget who helped me get there,' he

added meaningfully, pouring himself some tea from the pot which the waiter had placed by his elbow.

Ivor exchanged a quick glance with Brian Lipman before replying. 'Eddie, we'll work our butts off to get this product off the ground,' he said with great firmness. 'Have no fear, we'll give Four Seasons a flying start. From then on, though, it'll be up to your press and television advertising campaign to move it off the shelves. But there's no reason why it shouldn't sell well enough to go national. After all, it's not too highly priced and we know it's got all the nutrients a dog needs.'

'Hope you're right, Ivor, because if Four Seasons fails, I doubt if I'll get the job. My guess would be that Nick Clee, the young guy looking after sundries – leads, collars, food bowls and all that stuff – will be shunted sideways and I happen to know that his Uncle Louis is a director of Baum and Whitaker Public Relations.'

'I see what you're driving at,' said Ivor drily. 'Well, we'll all sink or swim together, Eddie. Now I have to choose the two girls we're going to use out of the four the agency is sending round this morning. It shouldn't take more than half an hour and I thought that Brian could take some photographs of you for the file whilst you're waiting.'

'By all means, shall we meet in the suite where we're holding the press conference?'

'Yes, that's fine, I'll see you there. Brian, if Mrs Rokeby and her dogs turn up early, make her comfortable and take a few shots of Huckleberry Hound or whatever the mutt's name is.'

'Charlie,' said Brian helpfully. 'Don't forget that, Ivor, you know what these breeders are like, they love their dogs like their own children.'

Eddie Taylor nodded vigorously and said: 'Or even

more, because animals are sometimes more lovable than kids because they don't answer back! But it's wrong to be cynical about people who keep pets just because we're in the business of selling to them. The latest medical research shows that keeping household animals reduces the chances of contracting stress-related illnesses like high blood pressure, heart attacks and strokes.'

'Stroking a pet reduces blood pressure and heart rate and just touching a responsive living animal fulfils a need for lots of lonely people,' added Ivor.

Brian Lipman was impressed and as he picked up his bag containing his equipment he remarked that he wouldn't mind having a dog at home.

'Well, why don't you get one, or doesn't Katie like dogs?' asked Ivor.

'She doesn't like Alsatians and I don't either,' he replied. 'I've always had the feeling that given half a chance an Alsatian would fancy having a go at you. No, if we had a pet, Katie would probably like a cat. I prefer dogs though, they're much more affectionate and they don't scratch the furniture or bring dead mice and birds into the house. Mind, I swore I'd never have a dog after what happened to me last year.'

Ivor glanced at his watch and winked at Eddie Taylor as he said: 'Go on, Brian, we've got five minutes to spare, let's hear all the gory details. We could all do with a laugh before we begin work.'

'What makes you so sure it's a funny story?' demanded the photographer, but from the smile which was playing around his lips it was obvious that the recollection was hardly painful for him. 'Anyhow, it's a bit near the knuckle and I wouldn't want to offend our client.'

Eddie Taylor quickly assured him that any such worries were unfounded. 'Have no fear, Brian, so long as it doesn't involve shagging sheep or little boys, I'd love to hear your story.'

'No problem there,' Brian grinned as he dropped his bag back on the floor. 'I've been called many things in my time, but never a shirtlifter. Hand on my heart, I've never fancied Larry the Lamb!

'No, this little affair happened last summer. I was staying overnight with Trish and Leon Standlake, some married friends of mine at their weekend cottage in Oxfordshire. There was another guest, Charlene Embleton, a gorgeous young American fashion model from San Francisco. Leon had met her a few weeks before at a party in California. I should explain that Leon's an international financial consultant and he's always flying round the world at the drop of a hat, the lucky sod. You can take my word for it, boys, Charlene was a stunner – fine silky hair so blonde that it was almost white, dazzling blue eyes, pretty face and a sumptuous figure, beautiful large breasts and a nice peachy bum. Leon told me that Hugh Hefner had offered her telephone numbers to pose for *Playboy* but so far she'd turned him down.

Ivor turned to Eddie Taylor and said solemnly: 'Well, she must have been something special to excite you, Brian. After all, you spend most of your time photographing luscious naked women all thirsting to wrap themselves round you.'

'Oh sure, sure. I can't even sit down for a tea break without some teenage dolly bird tearing open my trousers and pasting her lips round my love trunk – in my dreams, that is! And if I were dreaming about being plated, it would be by a girl like Charlene. I mean, it's true enough that I shoot an occasional nudie spread for the men's magazines so you could say I'm a bit *blasé* – but Charlene really made my eyes water.

16

'Anyhow, Trish cooked a lovely roast beef dinner and Leon opened two bottles of his 1961 Chateau Mouton Rothschild. We were feeling nice and replete when we toddled off into the lounge at about ten o'clock. A girl from the village had come in to wash up so the four of us were able to sit down for a game of bridge. I partnered Charlene against our hosts and sitting opposite the girl, I could hardly take my eyes off her. Now at first when I felt her toes brush my ankle, I thought she was just finding somewhere comfortable to rest her foot. But when she started to move her foot further up my leg, I lost my concentration and almost buggered up a lay-down three no trumps.'

'That would have been a terrible thing to do,' said Eddie, who was a keen bridge player, 'lifelong friendships have foundered on such mistakes.'

'Well, it's not easy trying to count how many hearts are still out when a pretty girl's toes are inching further and further up towards your cock,' retorted Brian defensively. 'But somehow I made the game and looked across at Charlene who was sitting there with a sweet innocent look on her face, like butter wouldn't melt in her mouth. Anyhow, she left me alone whilst we played the next hand. Leon had bid six spades, and though Charlene and I made the best defence, we couldn't take more than one trick and had to concede the rubber.'

'Sounds rather rude already,' said Ivor, whose prowess at cards was limited to poker and pontoon.

Brian Lipman ignored the interruption and continued: 'It was almost midnight and as we planned to go for a hike through the fields the next morning, we decided to finish the game and go to bed. It was a warm evening so I didn't bother to slip on my pyjamas even though I'd kept my window open whilst I lay on my bed reading a copy of

Vogue which I'd picked up the day before from Leon's library. Then I heard the floorboards creaking outside my room and I could see my door handle quietly turning and the door opening very, very slowly . . .'

He paused for dramatic effect and seeing that he had the full attention of his audience he went on: 'I put down the book and was about to reach for my dressing gown which was on a chair beside me when I saw who was making a late-night visit to my bedroom.

'It was none other than Charlene standing in the doorway, wearing a very transparent, very short pink nightie. And as her figure was silhouetted against the light, it was also clear that she wasn't wearing anything underneath! The light on the landing showed to perfection the beautiful curves of her breasts, her shapely figure and the fluffy triangle of golden hair between her legs.

'"Hi Brian, I hope I didn't startle you but I wasn't sure whether or not you'd still be awake," she explained as she gently closed the door behind her. "I couldn't sleep and thought to myself that if you weren't too tired, we could chat for a while. I know you don't do much fashion work but I'm sure you could help guide me through the London scene."

'"I'd like nothing better," I said, hastily sitting up and throwing the dressing gown over my lap. "I do some catalogue shots for various firms in the rag trade, but none of the high-class designer houses for which you work."

'"Never mind," she said and she came over and sat on the edge of the bed. "Oh, you're reading *Vogue*. May I have a look?" I gave her the magazine and she flipped through the pages till she came to a spread of a tall, leggy redhead who was modelling the new Christian Dior autumn outfits. "I know that girl, it's Shella de Souza, I worked with her in the Caribbean last year." As she leaned forward excitedly to concentrate on the photograph, she gave me a perfect view down the front of her nightie.

'God, what a sight! A pair of rounded red nipples, very hard and pointed. Up to now, the shock of her surprise appearance had inhibited the old libido, but the sight of these perfect tits made my cock rise up to the occasion. It wasn't easy to conceal my erection because it was covered only by the thin material of my dressing gown.

'My prick was getting harder all the time whilst she sat flicking through the pages of the magazine. Charlene made no attempt to move away when I put my arm across her shoulders and asked her if she were feeling a little cold. "Oh no," she said in her soft, sweet Californian accent. "If anything I'm rather warm. In fact I think I'll follow your example!" Before I could even reply, she got up and pulled her nightie over her shoulders and stood in front of me totally nude.

'Charlene looked at me with a quizzical expression on her face and then she murmured: "I think I'll be even more comfortable if I sit on your nice strong thighs." Quick as a flash, she pulled away my dressing gown and parked herself on my knees, facing me as she made herself comfortable. Then she glanced down on my stiffie which was waving wildly up in the air in front of her. She looked me in the eyes as she licked her lips and smiled as she circled her fingers around my cock and very gently began to toss me off.

'She leaned forward and kissed me and as we started to slide our tongues in each other's mouths, Charlene's hand slicked up and down my cock faster and faster as she worked her bum back and forth on my thighs.

'"Slow down or I'll come all over the place," I gasped as she continued this delicious wank. She slid off my knees to kneel in front of me. "There won't be any evidence," she whispered and her head went down and I felt her lovely wet lips close around my knob.

'I must be dreaming, I thought. I pinched myself on the arm but no, I was awake all right and the silky blonde mass of hair bobbing to and fro between my legs was no illusion. Charlene moved her head rhythmically back and forth, sucking at least half of my throbbing chopper into her mouth, lashing my raging tool with her tongue. Then she let my prick slip out of her mouth, which was just as well for otherwise I would have shot my load in seconds. She kissed my cock and tongued my shaft before sliding her head down and giving both my balls a little suck. Then she transferred her attentions to my helmet and she lapped all round it before taking the whole of my cock back inside her soft mouth.

'This time Charlene managed to suck it deep into her throat, all the way up to the base. She sucked away like mad and within a few moments, I spunked inside her mouth, but she continued to gobble my dick till every drop of jism had squirted down her throat.

'"I hope you're not finished for the night," she said as she gave my shrinking prick a farewell kiss and scrambled onto the bed. I looked at Charlene, lying on her back with her legs wide apart, and though I was desperate to fuck the lovely girl, my cock was totally limp. But I needn't have worried because before being fucked, she first asked me if I would eat her pussy.

'She didn't have to ask twice! I could clearly see her puffy love lips through her fluffy blonde bush. They were slightly open and had a pinkish glow about them and I dived down, spread her legs apart and kissed her clitty, rubbing my chin across her crack and forcing my tongue as far into her cunny as I could. Then I started to twirl my tongue around her clitty and the faster I vibrated it, the more excited we both became. Charlene gyrated like a girl possessed, arching her body in ecstasy as I pressed the tip of my tongue against her erect little button. My cock had now stiffened up again and I was just about to move myself up and slide my throbbing tool inside her warm, wet cunt when I fancied I heard the sound of the door opening behind me.

'I must have imagined it, I thought, as I heaved myself up and Charlene grabbed hold of my cock to guide it home. But then Benjie, Leon's golden retriever, jumps on the bed and starts sniffing my bum! Charlene hadn't closed the door properly and Benjie always roamed the house at night to see if he could find a bed to sleep in – a basket wasn't good enough for that bloody dog! Well, I don't know if you guys have ever tried to fuck whilst an over-friendly hound is washing his tongue on your buttocks, but I'll lay odds that you would find it as much a passion killer as I did!

'Charlene felt the same way too, from the minute she felt Benjie bounce up on the bed. All thoughts of how's-your-father were forgotten and even though I chucked the bloody dog off, he looked up at her so appealingly with those big, brown eyes that she made me let him jump back up again and he got more cuddles than I did for the next ten minutes. Then she suddenly looked at her watch and said that she had better slip back to her room as it was late and we were supposed to get up early the next morning. And as Charlene was leaving for London after tea, there was no further opportunity for us to finish what we'd started. To add insult to injury, her agency whisked her off to Paris a few days later and I haven't seen her since.'

The photographer finished his story with a heavy sigh and Eddie Taylor remarked: 'Bloody hell, I would have been very heavily tempted to slip some weedkiller into Benjie's bowl before I left.'

'Something like that did cross my mind,' Brian admitted. 'But Trish and Leon were nuts about the dog so the only revenge I could take was during the next day when I accidently on purpose kicked Benjie in the balls whilst I was bringing my bags downstairs.'

The head waiter sidled up to the table and murmured to Ivor that a Mr Campbell was waiting for him in the lobby. 'Thank you,' said Ivor and he pushed back his chair and stood up. 'Jimmy's arrived with the girls, so I'll ferry them up to the Burton suite. Brian, will you bring Eddie up there after you've taken the photographs of him that we were talking about? Gentlemen, I'll see you anon.'

Down in the bustling reception area Ivor looked around for Jimmy Campbell, with whom he had spoken on the telephone but had never met in person. He soon picked out his quarry, a short, dapper young man busily laying down the law to a little circle of attractive girls who were listening intently to him. Ivor slid through the circle, stretched out his hand and introduced himself. 'Jimmy Campbell? I'm Ivor Belling of Cable Publicity.'

'Ivor, great to meet you at last,' said the managing director of the Dolly Birds Model agency as he pumped Ivor's hand. 'All well for this morning? As you see, I've brought five of my best girls for you to choose from. Let me introduce Angela, Maggie, Ruth, Suzie and Vicky.'

Ivor smiled a greeting at the girls, who were all dressed in clothes which ensured admiring glances from the businessmen and other male guests who passed them by. Angela and Ruth were both wearing tight-fitting short minidresses with shiny white boots whilst Maggie, Suzie and Vicky favoured the new hot pants craze which well suited their long shapely legs.

'Thanks for coming, girls, I wish we could use you all. Let's go up to the suite we're using this morning and get cracking,' he said as he headed the procession up the stairs to the first floor.

In the Burton suite, the banqueting manager was supervising the layout for Cable Publicity's function. Rather than have his audience sitting in regimented rows, Ivor had asked for tables and chairs to be dotted round the room, with a space in front of the speaker's rostrum where, hopefully, Mrs Rokeby's dog Charlie would demonstrate how he preferred a tin of Four Seasons to any other canned dog food on the market. 'Ah, Mr Belling, is everything in order?' asked the manager and Ivor looked approvingly round the suite. 'Yes, that's just how I wanted everything arranged. Thank you very much, Mr Bell.'

The hotel staff withdrew and Jimmy Campbell suggested that he and Ivor should sit down. The girls would walk across the floor in front of their table and Ivor could ask any questions he wished to put to them.

'Carry on, Jimmy,' agreed Ivor and fished out a ball-point and a pad from the folder he was carrying. Jimmy called out to the girls to line themselves up once they had finished making the final touches to their make-up. Then he turned to Ivor and muttered: 'Your costumes are size tens, aren't they? Then they'll fit any of the girls. It makes no difference to me who you pick so I won't try to influence you at all. But as you'll see for yourself, Suzie will bulge in the right places.'

Ivor looked across at Suzie, a pneumatic auburn-haired girl whose shapely figure certainly took the eye. But it was the mini-skirted Ruth who was the first to saunter across. She was the youngest of all the girls, a svelte, long-legged seventeen year old whose pretty rounded face was ringed by a mop of curly strawberry-blonde hair.

She smiled seductively at Ivor as she sashayed past the table and he called out: 'Hi Ruth, have you ever done this kind of work before?'

'Oh yes, I was one of the hostesses at the Business Efficiency exhibition in Glasgow in March, so I'm used to dealing with people and passing out business information,' she replied. Jimmy Campbell muttered: 'Aye, there was quite a lot of business but not that much efficiency, if you get my drift. Ruthie's a super girl, she may look as if butter wouldn't melt in her mouth but when a couple of her bosses at this exhibition took a fancy to her, I don't think she ran too hard, if you take my drift.'

'Good to know,' mused Ivor, for a friendly girl could make all the difference to the tone of a journalist's copy.

'How would you feel about walking a dog, Ruth?' he asked and she beamed back a flashing smile. 'I love animals, Mr Belling. I have my own dog and I walk him every day in Queen Margaret Gardens.'

'Okay, thank you,' said Ivor and he scribbled down eight out of ten against Ruth's name. Jimmy nudged his arm and said: 'Now have a good look at Vicky, she's one of the most professional girls on our books.'

'So I see,' murmured Ivor as Vicky walked seductively across the floor, clad in a light grey sweater through which the points of her perky breasts pressed invitingly against the fine material. A pair of equally tight-fitting red velvet hot pants hugged the contours of her curvy backside which she wiggled suggestively at Ivor as she twirled round in front of him.

'Christ, I have to make a phone call,' Jimmy Campbell suddenly muttered. 'Ivor, would you excuse me for five minutes of so?'

'Of course,' replied Ivor and the agent hurried out of the room. Vicky tossed back her mane of black silky hair and said: 'What would you like to ask me?'

'I don't really know – except maybe to ask how you manage to get into those wonderful hot pants. They look as if they've been pasted on to you,' Ivor said with a grin.

'And very sexy they look too,' he added hastily although the girl was obviously not offended in the slightest by his remark. She returned his grin and said: 'I don't know about Maggie but Suzie and I bought ours at Scoobies, a new boutique that's just opened up in Renfield Street. She looks good in her pants, doesn't she? Suzie, come over here and let Mr Belling give you the once-over.'

Suzie strolled across to join them and Ivor was made very aware of what Jimmy Campbell had told him as they had sat down. Suzie's curves were certainly something special and he was forced to cross his legs as his shaft began to uncurl and swell up at the sight of the rise and fall of Suzie's thrusting breasts beneath her white linen blouse.

She stood directly in front of him and Vicky slipped her hand round her friend's waist and said coaxingly: 'We work best together, Mr Belling. And we don't mind putting on a show for your best customers afterwards either.'

'That's good to know, I won't forget it. Thank you girls!' said Ivor, who concealed his bewilderment, and he wrote eight against both their names in his notepad.

'Next please,' he called out and it was the buxom miniskirted Angela's turn to parade up and down, swinging her hips. Attractive as she was, she did not seem to put as much effort into her audition as the other girls and Ivor marked her down for only seven points.

'Super, and now Maggie, what have you got to offer?'
Ivor called out and the lithe girl swung off the table upon
which she had been perched and smoothed her hands
down her Lincoln green hot pants. She moved lazily
across the room and Ivor immediately recognised in her
gait the poise and self-assurance which was just what he
was looking for in the girls he wanted to hire. Ten out of
ten, he thought, for Maggie was also stunningly sexy, with
long strands of light chestnut hair framing her flawless
bronzed complexion and large dark brown eyes.

'How keen are you on animals?' he demanded and
Maggie rolled her tongue around her mouth sensuously
before answering: 'Grilled, boiled or fried?'

Ivor chuckled and said: 'I'm talking about dogs actually
– they might give you a straight answer to your question in
South Korea but I don't think our clients would want to
hear too much on those lines. Have you had any dealings
with press around here?'

She nodded and said: 'One of my boy friends is a
photographer on the *Evening Express*. He's taken some
pin-up shots of me which the paper's used as fillers in the
early editions.'

'Great,' said Ivor and he drummed his fingers on the
table. How the hell did he choose two out of these five
gorgeous girls? But fortunately for him, Vicky provided
the solution. 'Can I have a wee word?' she asked softly
and drew him to one side. 'Look, Jimmy told us what you
need us for. Why not use Suzie and me for the meet and
greet job and let Maggie and Ruth parade the hounds
round Glasgow? Angela won't be that bothered, she
starts four days work on a mail-order catalogue tomorrow
so she won't be that worried about it.'

Ivor gnawed at his upper lip as he quickly reviewed the
situation. This plan would mean going over budget but if

the launch was a success, Eddie Taylor would be pleased and the account would be safe for a fair time. So his boss, Martin Reece, wouldn't be too upset even if he was chary of passing on the cost of two extra girls to the client.

He made his decision and patted Vicky on the shoulder. 'All right, I'll go along with that idea,' he said firmly as the door opened and Jimmy Campbell walked briskly towards him. 'Sorry to have left you, Ivor, but I had to contact someone by half past ten. Well, have you made up your mind who you want?' he asked.

'Yup, you'll be pleased to know that I'd like to book Vicky and Suzie for the press conference and I'd like Maggie and Ruth to hand out the leaflets, though I don't suppose I'll get a volume discount.'

'Och, Cable wouldn't want to take bread out of the mouths of poor young girls,' said Mr Campbell with a worried expression. To his relief Ivor did not press the point, for although he was a firm believer in bargaining hard, Ivor always preferred to leave a margin for goodwill. For the sake of a few pounds, he would rather keep on the best terms with his suppliers in case he needed a favour from the Dolly Birds agency in the future.

'Maggie and Ruth had better try on the costumes now,' said Ivor. 'They're hanging in my wardrobe so we might as well pop up now and make sure all is well. If there are any alterations, the hotel housekeeper can give us a hand.'

'That won't be necessary, I'm a dab hand with a needle,' cooed Maggie.

'Vicky and Suzie, would you mind waiting till we come back?' Ivor went on. 'My photographer, Brian Lipman, will be here in a few minutes with Mr Eddie Taylor. He's the client so please be very nice to him.'

'Brian Lipman, did you say? Why, I know him, we've worked together before,' said Suzie brightly.

'Great! Jimmy, are you off too? I'll see you later perhaps. Girls, order yourself some coffee and biscuits or whatever takes your fancy. They'll be setting up a bar in the corner soon as we'll have the press here and you know how some of those journalists drink.'

'Aye, rather than bother with glasses you should just have two or three self-service petrol pumps on hand!' agreed Vicky. 'We'll be fine and don't fret, I promise we'll be awfully nice to Mr Taylor, won't we, Suze?'

With that, Ivor shepherded Maggie and Ruth up to his room on the next floor. Thankfully, Chrissie had departed whilst Ivor was having breakfast and the chambermaids had already swiftly tidied up the not inconsiderable mess which Chrissie and Ivor had left behind. He heard the girls whispering and giggling about something as he ruffled through the clothes in his wardrobe and pulled out the two bright red and green mini-dresses and said: 'Not exactly *haute couture*, I'm afraid, but these are the colours of the Four Seasons tins. I think one dress is slightly fuller than the other. Er, would you like to slip them on and make sure they fit?'

'Sure, why not?' said Ruth, as she lifted her arms to fiddle with the hook of her dress at the back of her neck. 'I'll go first and see if one of them looks okay on me.'

She finally managed to unhook her dress and Maggie assisted her pretty friend by pulling the zip down for her. Ivor gulped hard when Ruth let the dress fall away from her for the young teenager was wearing no bra and he gazed at her perky, high tipped, naked breasts. She was wearing only a tiny pair of frilly bikini panties through which Ivor could easily make out the shell-like outline of her cunny lips.

Ruth moved across and took one of the dresses from his trembling hands and slipped it over her head. 'This fits perfectly,' she said as she looked at herself in the long wall mirror. She pulled down the hem which barely covered her small, deliciously rounded bottom and giggled: 'It's a wee bit on the short side but I don't think the photographers will mind a little bit, will they?'

'No, not in the slightest,' said Ivor hoarsely. He turned round to Maggie who was sitting on the bed with the front of her pants already unbuttoned and added: 'Will you try yours on, too?'

'Of course,' said the sultry girl, sliding the clinging shorts down her legs. They were so tight that her white knickers were also pulled down and Ivor was treated to the sight of her thick, hairy bush before she pulled them up again. Then she unbuttoned her blouse and to Ivor's disappointment, Maggie was wearing a half-cup bra over which her breasts spilled perhaps even more sensuously than if she had been bare breasted like Ruth.

Luckily, the second dress fitted Maggie like a glove and Ivor mopped his brow with relief because there was little doubt that the two girls would look great for the cameras. 'I've got satin sashes with Four Seasons on them and of course, you'll each have a dog to look after – which reminds me, we'd better be getting back as the dog lady will be here soon with the hounds.'

'Oh dear, are you in a huge rush, Mr Belling? There was something which we wanted to find out,' said Ruth as she sidled round to stand beside him. She took hold of his arm whilst Maggie sat down on the bed.

He consulted his watch and said: 'I suppose we've got a few minutes to spare, so fire away. But the name's Ivor. Only my doctor, dentist and bank manager know me as Mr Belling.'

Ruth's brown eyes sparkled as she said boldly: 'Well, just between ourselves, Ivor, Maggie and I would like to know if it's true what Suzie said to us just now about Brian Lipman, your photographer.'

Ivor laughed out loud and replied: 'Very probably, though I didn't hear what she said about him. Was it about his work for *Ram*?' The girls looked puzzled and he went on to explain: 'That's a rather naughty American men's magazine which uses a lot of Brian's work.'

'Do you mean nudie spreads?' demanded Maggie with interest. 'Suzie said that Brian shot some really raunchy photographs of her and he paid her cash there and then, straight after the shoot, which is terrific for us.'

'No tax or agency commission to be deducted,' commented Ivor as he allowed Ruth to propel him towards the bed where he sat down next to Maggie. Ruth perched herself on his other side and said: 'Well, you know what the agencies are like. I mean, Jimmy Campbell's not as bad as some agents, but by the time he sends out an invoice and the client actually pays, it can be four months after the job before we see any money.

'And Suzie told us that Brian paid her a hundred pounds and gave her a set of colour transparencies as well. Maggie and I would be interested for that kind of money – especially if the photos are only going to be used in America.'

'I could have a quiet word with Brian if you like,' said Ivor, who was beginning to feel like the meat in a sandwich as the two girls moved their soft bodies closer against him. 'Obviously, you wouldn't want Jimmy Campbell to know anything about it.'

'Oh, thank you, Ivor, we'd be very grateful,' said Maggie, kissing him lightly on his ear which made him shiver all over.

'Very, very grateful indeed,' said Ruth, following her friend's example. Ivor's heart began to race as the teenage girl moved her hand onto his thigh and let her fingers idly move across to stroke the bulge which had now formed in the lap of his trousers.

'Do you think he has a big cock?' enquired Maggie, and the timbre of her throaty, voluptuous voice made Ivor's tadger throb even more excitedly. He sat dumbfounded as Ruth replied: 'There's only one way to find out,' and with practised hands she unbuckled his belt and unzipped his fly. Her hand snaked inside the opening and she released his rock-hard erection which shot up to stand like a miniature flagpole out of his trousers.

'M'mm, not bad, not bad at all,' said Maggie admiringly. She clasped hold of his quivering cock and began massaging his swollen shaft, drawing back his foreskin and making the purple helmet swell and bound in her hand. 'For a Sassenach, that is,' she giggled. Ivor gasped as Maggie's head swooped down and she planted a loving wet kiss on his uncapped knob.

'I think Ivor has a very pretty cock,' said Ruth as she slid to her knees and moved herself in front of him. She cupped his hairy ballsack in her hands and bent her head down to begin licking the underside of his shaft whilst Maggie concentrated on giving his twitching helmet another quick moistening lick. Then she opened her mouth wide and took at least three inches of his palpitating prick between her lips as Ruth opened her mouth and sucked in one of his balls.

'Oh my God!' groaned Ivor who was in the seventh heaven of delight as Maggie's moist mouth worked its way along the length of his succulent shaft. She held the base of his prick as she pumped her head up and down, keeping her lips taut as she kissed and sucked his cock with evident enjoyment. Then she pulled her lips away to look at the pre-cum juice which was already oozing out of the tiny 'eye' on the top of his knob. Maggie guessed that he would be unable to hold back for much longer so she clamped her lips back over his knob and slurped noisily over the purple dome as Ruth continued to suck his balls.

Moments later Maggie was proved right as, with a hoarse cry, Ivor shot a fountain of foamy spunk inside her mouth. She rubbed his pulsating pole fiercely as she sucked and swallowed his jism, milking his cock of every last drop until she felt his member soften inside her mouth to a heavy semi-stiffness.

She looked up to him wide-eyed as she slowly disengaged her mouth from the fleshy tube. Holding Ivor's prick in her hand, she turned to her friend and offered it to her as she remarked: 'Your turn, Ruthie!' But before the girl could do more than wash her tongue over his knob, Ivor hastily pushed his prick back inside his trousers and zipped up his fly.

'Sorry, Ruth, I'd love you to suck my cock but we don't have the time,' he said regretfully. 'I have to go downstairs to welcome Mrs Rokeby, the lady who's bringing along the gourmet dog to the press conference and the two labradors who you'll be taking for a walk this afternoon. I think it best if you'd change back into your own clothes and then come back here to put the Four Seasons dresses on again in time to make the grand entrance for the photo-call at one forty five. Here, Maggie, I'll give you my key. Now, are there any questions?'

'Just one,' pouted Ruth, blowing him a kiss. 'When will you be able to fuck me with your big cock?'

'As soon as you come back from walking the dogs,' he promised with a wolfish smile. 'And I'll also have spoken to Brian Lipman by then and fixed things up for you both with him.'

'Thanks Ivor! Go on, you pop back to the suite and we'll follow you in five minutes, once we've changed and done up our faces,' said Maggie. He took up this suggestion and left the girls in his room whilst he made his way back to the Burton Suite.

A quick glance at the clock on the wall told him that it was now ten past eleven but Mrs Rokeby had not yet arrived and Brian Lipman was nowhere to be seen. This did not appear to have bothered Eddie Taylor who was sitting on a sofa flanked by Vicky and Suzie who were shrieking with laughter. 'Oh hi, Ivor,' said Suzie gaily. 'Eddie here has just told us a very funny joke.'

It hasn't taken long for Mr Taylor to become 'Eddie', thought Ivor, who briefly wondered whether Suzie or Vicky had given his client the same treatment as he had received upstairs. 'Can I hear it, I like a good story,' he said, and Eddie Taylor was happy to oblige. He cleared his throat and said: 'It's the one about the high-class girl from Edinburgh who gets undressed on her wedding night and climbs into bed stark naked except for a pair of white gloves. Her husband looks at her and says: "Darling, why have you left your gloves on?" and she says: "Well, Mummy said that I might have to touch the beastly thing!"'

Ivor smiled his appreciation and moved across the room to answer the ringing telephone which was behind the bar which had been set up whilst he was upstairs with Maggie and Ruth.

'Hello, is that you Ivor? It's me, Brian, I'm in reception with Mrs Rokeby and the dogs. I think you'd better come down to reception pronto,' said the photographer and he hung up.

'Brian says Mrs Rokeby and the dogs have arrived,' Ivor announced. 'I'll be back in a couple of minutes.'

'Take your time, there's no hurry,' said Eddie Taylor genially as he put his arms around the girls on either side of him. 'I'm being well looked after here.'

But not as well as me, muttered Ivor as he rapidly descended the staircase to reception. Brian Lipman was standing with a tallish, extremely attractive young woman in her mid to late twenties who was holding two golden labradors and a smaller tan coloured mongrel on leads.

Brian waved to him and made the introductions: 'Ivor, meet Beth Rokeby – Beth, this is Ivor Belling. You've not met before, have you?'

'No, we've not met though we've spoken on the phone,' said Ivor, shaking hands with the dog breeder as he flashed her a welcoming smile. Beth Rokeby in the flesh was nothing like the woman he had expected to see. He had imagined her to be a horse-faced woman with close-cropped hair in a tweed skirt who barked out orders to her dogs like a sergeant major on the parade ground. But instead he was looking at a pretty, rather winsome girl in a matching pink sweater and skirt. Although she was not wearing her skirt as high above the knee as the models from the Dolly Bird agency, it still showed to good effect her long, shapely legs.

'How nice to meet you at last,' she said in a sweet sibilant voice which had just a touch of a Highland burr in its timbre. 'I'm so sorry to tell you that we have a slight problem on our hands.'

'Don't tell me Charlie has gone off Four Seasons,' said Ivor, clapping his hand to his head in an exaggerated gesture.

Beth reassured him that Charlie would still do the business. 'No, he'll do as he's told. It's just that the reception people are making a fuss about allowing the dogs inside.'

'Oh, how ridiculous! The dogs won't be in any public rooms, though I don't want the labradors to be seen until the two girls who are walking round the town with them this afternoon make their entrance. Leave this to me.' Ivor turned angrily to the reception desk where a smooth-faced assistant manager was waiting for his attack.

Ivor explained the situation but the polite answer was that they had to comply with the new public health regulations and only guide dogs could be exempted from the ban. 'But of course, the dogs can be taken up to the Burton Suite, sir, so long as they stay there,' said the manager. Ivor scowled and then had a brainwave. 'Well, that will have to suffice, so long as you can put up a couple of screens that the dogs can stay behind. We don't need all the space, so if you partition off a corner of the room, we'll put the dogs behind them.'

'Would they sit quiet until we need them, Beth?' asked Brian.

'They've been well exercised this morning and I should think that all they'd like to do right now is have a nice nap,' she replied.

He exhaled deeply and turned back to the reception desk. 'Thank God for small mercies! Could I please ask you to have those screens put up immediately.'

'Certainly, Mr Belling,' said the manager, who was equally glad to end the dispute on a friendly compromise. 'I'll supervise the erection myself.'

'I'd rather have one of our models supervise mine,' murmured Brian softly but Beth Rokeby had sharp ears and she chuckled and said: 'You're using girls from Jimmy Campbell's Dolly Bird agency, aren't you? My brother has been going out with a girl named Maggie McKenzie who is on their books. I wonder if she'll be here today.'

'Your brother wouldn't be a press photographer by any

chance, would he?' asked Ivor as he led the way up the stairs.

'Yes, Ken's with the *Evening Express*. How did you know that?'

'Maggie's one of the girls we've hired and she mentioned that her boy friend was on the *Evening Express*,' said Ivor, hoping that Beth's brother was not a large muscular type who might be angry, to say the least, if he discovered that his girl friend was in the habit of sucking off her favoured clients!

So he was much relieved when Beth remarked: 'It's a small world, isn't it? Mind, I think "boy friend" is stretching things a bit because they live in a very free and easy manner and Ken goes out with other girls and Maggie with other boys, even though they spend most weekends together.'

Maggie and Ruth had returned from Ivor's bedroom so the entire company was present in the Burton Suite. After he had introduced Beth Rokeby, Ivor said: 'I'd like to run through the arrangements one more time. Now the press conference begins at noon so we must all be ready by eleven forty five – that's in just over twenty minutes time. Vicky and Suzie, I'd like you two to stand at the entrance and ask our guests to sign the visitors book and make sure they're all given one of the folders which are on the table by the door. Inside the folder there's a press release about Four Seasons, some grocery trade news, and a couple of photographs of the tins. Maggie and Ruth, would you just circulate and make sure no-one's looking lonely.

'Brian, you'll snap away and make sure we have shots of every trade guest, preferably in conversation with Eddie. Get one or two of the press folk which might be useful for us.

'Eddie, you'll look after the trade people and I'll take

care of the journalists. We'll be serving drinks till half past twelve and then I'll call the meeting to order and introduce you. Maggie and Ruth, that's when you two can slip away to change. Then when Eddie's finished extolling the praises of Four Seasons, I'll call on Beth who will bring on Charlie to do his stuff and then we'll answer any questions anyone might want to ask.'

He paused as the door opened and two men came in carrying a large screen. 'Could you put that partition round that corner of the room, please?' he called out, pointing out where he wanted it placed, and then went on: 'Maggie and Ruth, I'm afraid we're having a spot of bother with the hotel about the dogs, so we're going to put them behind that screen. When you come back here, slip in quietly and go behind the screen and stay there till you hear me call you. Then you come in with the dogs for the photo-call whilst we re-open the bar and we'll serve sandwiches and stuff till about two fifteen. Now what happens then, Eddie?'

'Young Kevin Dawson, my assistant will escort the girls round to Websters, a big new supermarket round the corner in Argyll Street where there's a huge window display of Four Seasons. The girls will give out the money-off coupons.'

'Good, and of course Brian and hopefully one or two press photographers will also go along too,' said Ivor, clicking his thumb and forefinger together as he recalled that Chrissie and Paula, his and Brian Lipman's bedmates from the previous evening, had worked at Websters. Brian had remembered too and he said: 'I've met a couple of girls who work there and they'll co-operate if we need any help.'

'Then they'll come back and if the weather holds up, which it should if the forecasters are to be believed, we'll go down to Newton Mearns and repeat the exercise there,' said Eddie Taylor.

Beth Rokeby raised her hand. 'I'll go on these trips too, if I may, as I don't like letting Honey and Archie out of my sight,' she said. Ivor nodded his agreement. 'Of course you can,' he said and he looked around the room. 'Now are there any questions? No? Well, good luck, everybody. We'll meet back here at eleven forty-five sharp.'

The meeting broke up and Eddie Taylor said to Ivor: 'I'm going downstairs to get a porter to help me bring in the tins of Four Seasons I have in the car to make up a nice display. No, I don't need any help, Kevin Dawson will be here any minute and he'll give me a hand.'

Beth Rokeby opened up a large carrier bag she had brought with her and said: 'I've got the bowls for the demonstration here and I'll ask someone to put down saucers of water for Honey and Archie behind the screen.'

Suzie came up and asked if the girls could leave their handbags in Ivor's bedroom. 'It's much easier for us than having to bother with cloakroom tickets and we can change and do our make-up without getting in anyone's way,' she explained.

'Be my guest,' he replied expansively. 'Maggie has the key but make sure she keeps it with her as she and Ruth have to go back to change into their outfits whilst Eddie is making his speech.'

'Thanks, Ivor,' chorused the girls. Brian Lipman left with them so that Ivor was left with only Beth Rokeby. He slumped down into a chair and tickled one of the labradors under the chin as the dog nuzzled its wet nose against his wrist.

'Are you tired already?' asked Beth Rokeby as she pulled up a chair to join him.

He shook his head and replied: 'Not really, it's just that the hour before an event is always a hairy time as far as I'm concerned. Have I covered all the bases? Will the press turn up? What coverage will we get and will the client be happy with it? I'm sure that advertising must be far easier work than public relations. Of course, you have to have the skill to put over the message but at least with adverts, the space is paid for so you know where and when what you've written will appear.'

'But advertising is expensive, isn't it? I know it costs a fortune to buy TV time, although thank goodness the pet food people are hooked on television because I supply quite a few dogs for the commercials.'

'So your kennels aren't just a hobby?'

'Well, it began that way but now it's a full-time business, and I have two kennel-maids working part-time for me.'

'Your husband's not in the business then?'

'Ex-husband,' she corrected him gently. 'Roger and I parted last year.'

Ivor grimaced and apologised to her for making her disclose a personal matter. 'Sorry, I didn't mean to cross-examine you,' he said, but Beth Rokeby had not taken any offence at his questioning. 'That's alright, Mr Belling, you weren't to know and anyhow, it's not like a death, it so happens that I kicked him out exactly twelve months ago next Saturday.'

He repeated the remark he had made to Maggie and Ruth about his preference for being called Ivor and she flashed him a wide, welcoming smile. 'I'm Beth,' she said and she continued: 'Yes, I'll have my divorce decree any day now as Roger's not contesting it. Not that he could, of course, without having to explain the embarrassing circumstances of why I left him.'

'Oh dear,' said Ivor with suitable regret in his voice. 'Was it a case of *cherchez la femme*?'

Beth gave a short laugh and said: 'No, though I think it might have been easier to cope with the split if there had been another woman involved. I don't say I would have stayed with him because in my opinion, adultery's a serious breach of trust. Are you married, Ivor?'

'No, but I agree with you,' he replied sincerely. 'If you're single or separated, that's one thing, but it's not right to cheat on your partner.'

'I wish more men felt like you,' Beth said as she let the dogs' leads fall from her hands and as she had predicted, they curled up to lie still by her feet. 'But with Roger I was cheated twice over, so to speak.'

Ivor said nothing but waited for her to continue. He guessed, correctly, that she was still hurt by what had happened and found some comfort by talking about it. So he was not surprised when Beth continued: 'Yes, it still annoys me when I think about what happened. Roger's from Charlestown, a village near Aberdeen, and he's always been a countryman at heart even though he's an architect by profession. I met him at a Young Liberals dance in Edinburgh when I was nineteen and he was twenty-one. I was working as a legal secretary and breeding labradors as a hobby at the time. Anyhow, Roger took me home, we started dating and we got married just before my twenty-first birthday.'

Beth sighed at the memory before she went on: 'I should have guessed that there was something a wee bit different about Roger whilst we were courting. I mean, I'd been out with boys since I was fifteen and they've all wanted to kiss and cuddle as far as I'd let them go, if you know what I mean. But even when we were engaged, I sometimes found myself taking the lead when we were petting on the sofa when we'd come back from the pictures and my parents had gone to sleep. Perhaps the fact that Roger was such a gentleman was part of the attraction, and all was well on the wedding night though soon afterwards I should have realised his true nature.'

She dropped her voice. Ivor hunched his shoulders and leaned forward as Beth continued: 'I couldn't understand why Roger liked to take me from behind. At first he joked about it saying that he saw the dogs do it that way and they seemed to enjoy themselves. I was quite happy about that except that doggie-style is a very impersonal way of making love, especially for a newly-wed couple.

'Then he tried to, ah, um –'

Ivor quickly saved her any embarrassment. 'Go up the tradesmen's entrance,' he suggested with a little smile and she threw him a grateful look. 'Precisely,' she agreed, 'and I wasn't happy about *that* at all!' Ivor nodded with real sympathy for whilst he was not averse to an occasional tight bum-hole and although he knew several girls who enjoyed the experience, he always held that the best love-making happened only when both partners were fully happy with whatever was being attempted.

She wrinkled her nose and carried on: 'To be fair, he didn't try to force me once I'd made it clear that I didn't go in for that sort of thing. But more often than not, when we went to bed at night, all we did was sleep!

'I went to see the doctor and when I complained to him that Roger only made love to me once a week the old fool had the nerve to tell me that I was over-sexed! Well, that was on a Friday and the very next day I found out what was really the trouble.

'Roger was the leader of the local group of boy scouts in the small village about five miles outside Edinburgh where we lived. On Saturday afternoons he would often take the lads hiking or whatever in the country. Well, that Saturday afternoon, I took out my dogs for a walk and I saw three of the boys from Roger's troop waiting at the bus stop. "Hi there," I said as I approached them, "are you bunking off Scouts this afternoon?"

'"No, Mrs Rokeby," one of them said to me. "There's no Scouts' meeting today so we're off to the cinema instead." That's odd, I thought, so I put the dogs back on their leads and walked the mile or so to Farmer MacFarlane's old barn where I knew the scouts met. When I got there, there was no noise coming from inside the barn, so I opened the door quietly and got the shock of my life. Fred Brown, the butcher's boy and deputy scoutmaster, was leaning against a post. He was dressed in his uniform but with his shorts pulled down and Roger was on his knees sucking his prick! They hadn't heard me come in and I stood silently for a moment and watched Roger play with Fred's balls till the young man spurted into Roger's mouth.

'Then one of the dogs started barking and when Roger saw me he shouted out: "My God, it's Beth! What the hell are you doing here?" and he began to shake all over with fear. "You'd better go home," I said curtly to him and he didn't say another word but slunk out of the barn.'

'What about young Fred? Christ, he must have been almost as embarrassed as your husband,' commented Ivor.

'No, strangely enough he wasn't. Fred simply stood there coolly, not even bothering to cover himself up. I couldn't help noticing how well-endowed he was for a lad of seventeen. "Don't you know that what you were up to is against the law?" I said sternly but he shrugged his shoulders and said with some insolence. "Yes, and it's a pretty unfair law at that. If I were having sex with a willing girl there would be no problem, so why can't I fool around with a man?"

'I suppose there was a certain logic in his words but I had the notion that he was not totally queer. This thought was proved correct when he caught me staring at his prick which was so surprisingly big for a lad of his age. He leered at me as he cupped his cock in his fist and rubbed it up and down until it stood stiff and hard against his lean belly. "I'd far prefer to fuck you, Mrs Rokeby, than play around with your husband – even though he gives me such nice presents."

'I said nothing as he continued to stroke himself and the cheeky boy grinned at me and said: "Doesn't this turn you on?" He closed his eyes and he jerked his hand up and down faster. It took only a few more tugs before he arched his back and grunted loudly as his cum jetted out of his cock, the first splatter just missing me as the rest dribbled over his knuckles and down between his fingers.

'One of the dogs started barking and I turned on my heel and walked straight back home where Roger was waiting for me. He was in a shocking state, trembling all over and pacing up and down the room because he was terribly worried that I might tell the police about what I'd seen. I have to admit that this had crossed my mind. But instead I decided that if Roger would not contest a divorce and come to a fair financial settlement, then I would say nothing to the authorities. He agreed immediately to my terms and actually, since we split up, we've become quite good friends.

'Now this may sound priggish, but I also warned Roger that though his secret would be safe with me, he would be well advised to keep away from young men such as Fred Brown who might be disposed to blackmail him.'

'Very sound advice, if I may say so,' murmured Ivor,

who was only too aware of the perils facing homosexuals. One of Cable Publicity's clients, a well-known pop star, was gay and his manager was constantly concerned that this might leak out to the press.

'Roger now lives in Edinburgh with a man of a similar persuasion, but I've not found anyone else. I'm in no hurry to settle down again but that doesn't mean to say that I want to live like a nun,' said Beth Rokeby, placing her hand on Ivor's thigh.

'I wouldn't have thought you'd be given a chance to find out,' he said as he ran his fingertips along the top of her hand.

'You'd be surprised, Ivor,' she said, squeezing his thigh sensuously before removing her hand. 'I sometimes wonder whether the dogs put them off but my lot wouldn't hurt a fly. They're too gentle, really. If a burglar came in the house, Charlie would lick him to death.'

'Yes, though dogs can put some men off their stride,' said Ivor with a smile. 'If you get the chance, you must ask Brian, my photographer, about his experiences with a certain golden retriever named Benjie.'

At this point the bulky figure of Eddie Taylor came in closely followed by a sandy-haired young man who manoeuvred a trolley piled high with cardboard boxes through the swing doors. 'This is Kevin, one of my assistants, and he's brought up all the tins we need for a display. We've also got cans of the other leading brands too.'

Beth Rokeby rose from her seat and said: 'I've got the bowls here for Charlie's demonstration. Now, Eddie, this is very important, whatever you do, make sure that you spoon out the Four Seasons into the blue bowl. I suggest you make a line of the bowls and you can plonk Charlie down on either end or in the middle. You can even ask one of the guests to change the order of the bowls if they want to, it won't matter, Charlie will make for the blue bowl every time.'

'Why is that, Beth?' asked Ivor curiously and she wagged a reproving finger at him. 'It's really a trade secret, but I'll give you a clue. Does the name Pavlov mean anything to you?'

'He was a Russian psychologist, wasn't he?' hazarded Eddie Taylor.

'Quite right, and he studied conditioned reflexes in dogs, especially how they can be trained to recognise signals which herald food.'

'So Charlie associates the blue bowl with food?' said Ivor but Beth shook her head. 'No, most dogs are colour blind to some extent. But there's a distinctive smell to the blue bowl because every day I rub in some special ointment. Our noses can hardly pick it up, but dogs have a much better sense of smell than we have and Charlie associates that smell with his favourite food, so ninety nine times out of a hundred, he'll always choose to eat tinned food from the blue bowl even if there's fresh chopped butcher's meat in another bowl next to it.'

'Well, let's pray that the one-in-a-hundred wrong choice won't happen today,' muttered Ivor as he mopped his brow.

Beth winked at the two men and said: 'It won't I promise you, because just to make sure, I've lightly coated the other bowls with castor oil.'

'You're a girl after my own heart,' said Eddie Taylor happily and he went off to help Kevin Dawson set up the display.

Brian Lipman and the four Dolly Bird girls now came in and Ivor rubbed his hands together. 'Okay everyone, ready to go? Take your places, the show's about to begin!'

❀ TWO ❀

I Love A Lassie

At twenty to one Ivor permitted himself to heave a sizeable sigh of satisfaction. So far, so good, he said to himself whilst he scanned the audience who were listening to Eddie Taylor extol the merits of feeding Four Seasons to man's best friend. To his and Eddie's great relief, all the trade customers had arrived safely and the most important buyer there, Giles Horrobin, was obviously so taken with Vicky's sultry charms that he would have gladly volunteered to eat a cream cracker dipped in Four Seasons if the sexy girl had asked him to do so.

Furthermore, every popular national newspaper had sent along a reporter and a photographer. The signatures of journalists from the *Glasgow Herald* to the *Scottish Daily Sketch* would look very impressive in the visitors' book which Ivor could show his client. Ken Barret, Beth Rokeby's brother and Maggie's boy friend, was one of the four photographers who were fixing their flashlights in preparation for the promised demonstration. The appearance of the scantily dressed pretty girls was all their editors would be interested in, so long as there was a news peg of some kind which could be used as a caption. All seemed to be going to plan.

Eddie Taylor finished his sales pitch by introducing Beth Rokeby, 'one of Scotland's top breeders, who will help to demonstrate just how much dogs love this wonderful new product.' Beth came to the front with Charlie on his lead, and she asked one of the journalists in the front row if he would pick up the five bowls which were behind her and place them in any order on the floor. Then she gave Charlie's lead to the pressman and went over to a side table where five open tins of dog food were standing on a tray. To Charlie's evident pleasure, she lifted the tray and walked back and set it down in front of him. As she did so, Charlie yelped with delight and began to wag his tail furiously whilst at the back of the room, Maggie and Ruth slipped behind the screen having returned to the suite after changing into their garish Four Seasons outfits.

A smile spread over Ivor's face as he watched Beth empty half the contents of the Four Seasons tin into the blue bowl. She invited another journalist to spoon in similar amounts from the rest of the tins into the other bowls. Brian Lipman and the other photographer crowded round as Beth said: 'Now would anyone like me to move the bowl with the Four Seasons somewhere else in the line? Look, I'll move it to the very far side away from Charlie. We can't be fairer than that, can we?'

Brian Lipman hastily changed the film in his camera as Beth took Charlie off his lead and, holding his collar, led him through the audience to where Ivor was standing. Then she turned and released the dog which skipped back to the line of food bowls, sniffed the contents of the red and yellow ones and then moved to the blue bowl and began to guzzle the generous helping of Four Seasons as if he had not been fed for a week.

Silently, Ivor punched the air in jubilation and made his way up to the front table. Eddie Taylor led a round of applause whilst Beth pulled Charlie away from his feast.

'Ladies and gentlemen, I'd now like you to meet Ruth and Maggie who will be distributing half-price vouchers to shoppers in Argyll Street this afternoon,' announced Ivor. The two girls made a grand entrance with the labradors. To the delight of the photographers, neither girl was wearing a bra and Maggie's large creamy breasts looked to be in imminent danger of spilling completely out of her low cut dress. The photographers clustered round and urged Maggie to sit on her haunches and lean forward to pat her dog. This inevitably led to one bosom popping right out and though she knew full well what had occurred, Maggie waited for a few well-timed seconds before covering herself up.

Waiters now circulated with trays of drinks and Eddie Taylor clapped Ivor on the back. 'Well done, sir, everything's gone like clockwork,' Eddie enthused. 'We're bound to make the papers and on my side, all the big boys have told me that they'll give Four Seasons their full support. I've already taken extra orders from Bill MacFarlane and Graham Bowe.'

He dropped his voice and whispered: 'Look here, Ivor, that guy over there, Giles Horrobin, he buys pet foods for the biggest chain of supermarkets in Scotland. But believe it or not, he's asked *me* to have a late lunch with him and he's also invited Vicky to join us.'

'I'm not surprised,' said Ivor. 'I could see he was undressing her with his eyes the minute she gave him the launch folder.'

'Maybe, but she's accepted his invitation and I've asked Suzie to make up a foursome if that's okay with you.'

'Sure, the girls have done what was needed as far as I'm concerned and they can leave whenever they like. Now do you need anything else from me?'

Eddie blushed and muttered: 'Well, I can't believe we'll be that lucky, but Giles wants to eat here and dropped a heavy hint about having a bedroom available afterwards. I couldn't put that through on my expenses.'

'Not a bad idea, it's always best to be prepared,' said Ivor with a shrug. 'I'll be using mine as I've a report to write and some calls to make to the office. And I have a feeling that Brian might be busy as well. Tell you what, I'll book another room under your name on Cable's account. There'll be no problem, the hotel's only half full. You can pick up the keys at the reception desk and drop them back to me when you're ready to go.'

'Thanks, Ivor, I'm obliged to you,' said a relieved Eddie Taylor. 'However, much as Giles might hope to the contrary, I can't see us needing it. Just in case though, I've asked young Kevin to pack everything away and he'll go down to Websters with the two girls in about half an hour.'

'You never know your luck,' said Ivor as he looked across the room at Beth Rokeby's striking figure. 'For instance, I could be wrong but I have a sneaking feeling that I may be in with a fighting chance of establishing closer relations with Charlie's mistress.'

Eddie followed his gaze and murmured: 'Well, so long as he doesn't bite your bum when you're on the job like that hound which upset the apple cart for poor Brian Lipman.' Then he went off to make his final good-byes to the rest of his guests from the grocery trade.

It was time now for Ivor to check that the reporters had all the details they needed. He also offered sample tins of

Four Seasons to any dog owners amongst them, though this did not take long because all the information they could possibly need had been neatly provided in the press releases inside their folders.

After he had shepherded out the last guest, Brian Lipman called out to him: 'Ivor, there's no need for you to go to Argyll Street. It's only round the corner and I'll look after Ruth and Maggie with young Kevin here.'

'Are you sure?' said Ivor doubtfully but the photographer said: 'No sweat, honestly, why don't you take Beth out for a drink. Charlie did us proud, didn't he, but I don't think he particularly wants a gin and tonic.'

'No, he wouldn't, but I'd love one,' said Beth, who had heard Brian's suggestion as she piled her dog bowls back into a carrier bag.

Ivor looked steadily at her. 'I'd be more than happy to sink one with you, but I thought you would be going to Argyll Street as you never let your dogs out of your sight.'

'Well, I'm prepared to make an exception to the rule today because I know Maggie will take good care of them,' said Beth judiciously. 'My brother Ken is going to be there as well to take a few more pictures for the *Evening Express*. Then Brian and Kevin are going on to Newton Mearns in Kevin's car for your second give-away outside the Co-op.'

'We can take Charlie with us too,' said Brian as he bent down to put his camera in his case. He straightened up and went on: 'Kevin says we'll be back here at about four o'clock, so we'll see you in the coffee shop around then, is that okay?'

'Super,' said Ivor. Five minutes later, he was sitting down in the bar with Beth, congratulating himself on the good fortune which enabled him to be alone with the bewitching lady and also on the fact that he had reminded himself to reclaim the key of his bedroom from Maggie before she and Ruth left the hotel. He had offered Beth some lunch but she demurred, saying that she'd tucked into the delicious hot snacks and smoked salmon sandwiches which had been served at the press conference.

After the waitress had placed a second round of gin and tonics on their table, Beth said quietly: 'I'm surprised that you haven't asked me countless questions about a particular subject, Ivor. Most men do when I meet them. Can you guess what they might be?'

He considered the matter thoughtfully and said hesitantly: 'Must be something to do with the dogs, I suppose.'

'Well done! Of course I adore dogs, but I'm sure that out of hours you don't want to talk about public relations.'

'I certainly don't,' he agreed as he moved his chair nearer to her and deciding to ride his luck. 'There are many more interesting subjects to talk about, like when I'm going to be able to help you make up for all that lost time when you were married to Roger.'

'Lost time?' she echoed but when Ivor squeezed her hand she giggled and said: 'You're a quick worker, Mr Belling.'

'*Tempus fugit*, Mrs Rokeby,' he replied and he stood up and returned her smile adding: 'Shall we finish these drinks in a more private place?'

'Like your bedroom?' she said as she also rose from her chair.

'What a splendid idea! Why didn't I think of that!' said Ivor and holding their drinks precariously in their free hands, they marched arm in arm towards the lift.

Once safely inside Ivor's room they put down their drinks and Beth looked round with interest at the two dresses which were lying on the bed whilst Ivor took off his jacket. He caught her enquiring glance and he explained that they belonged to Maggie and Ruth who had used the room to change into their Four Seasons costumes. This mollified her and she put down her drink on the dressing table before sitting down on the bed.

'Maggie is a really lucky girl to have such lovely big bosoms,' said Beth ruefully as she pulled off her sweater to reveal two smallish but firm mounds which were cradled in the softly padded half-cups of a lacy beige bra. 'My boobs are on the small side,' she said regretfully as Ivor sat down next to Beth, slipping his arm round her slim waist as he gave her an affectionate cuddle.

'They're absolutely perfect for your body,' said Ivor. He held her close and they looked briefly at each other before they exchanged a brief kiss. For a moment there was an awkward silence but then she came into his arms and Ivor's cock began to thicken and swell. As they locked into a passionate embrace, he could feel Beth's tongue working frantically inside his mouth.

He slid the straps of her bra over her shoulders and she wriggled her arms free as he reached around and unclipped it. As it fell away from her body Beth let Ivor pull her fully onto the bed and she lay on her back moaning gently as he softly started to kiss the valley between her jutting breasts. Then with a sensuous smile she pulled his lips towards an erect, raspberry-red nipple.

He sucked it into his mouth and she gasped her arousal as she squirmed from side to side as Ivor licked and lapped at the rubbery morsel whilst he tore off his shirt and unbuckled his belt. He swirled his tongue round one trembling nipple whilst he kicked off his shoes and wrenched off his trousers and underpants in one quick movement, and then he pulled up his legs so that he could remove his socks and release himself from all his unwanted clothes.

At the same time Beth had unhooked the catch at the top of her skirt and pulled down the zip and now she lifted her bottom as Ivor tugged the skirt down to her feet. She kicked it away and raised her bottom a second time as Ivor rolled her panties over her thighs and knees and she pulled her right leg out of them leaving the frilly garment dangling over her left ankle.

'Oh, yes, yes, yes!' she gasped as Ivor's mouth now travelled downwards to the dark thatch of curly hair between her thighs. She parted her legs as he slurped a series of noisy wet kisses along the edges of her pouting pussy lips. Unlike several of his friends, Ivor enjoyed eating pussy and he fastened upon Beth's crack with relish. The girl quivered with delight whilst he forced his tongue inside her moistening honeypot. He probed her soaking slit with enthusiasm and before long her hips were bucking violently and her back was arching up from the mattress as he found her clitty and probed at it with his teeth.

'A-a-a-h! A-a-a-h! A-a-a-h!' she cried out as Ivor nipped at the erect little ball whilst his hands roved over her breasts, tweaking the stiff nipples until Beth shuddered all over as she climaxed with a rush of passion. She relaxed into limpness as the delicious crisis slowly melted away. But then after a few moments she placed her hands under his shoulders and helped him heave himself upwards until he was positioned above her, balancing his weight on the palms of his hands. Beth grasped his straining shaft and as he sank slowly down on top of her she guided it between her yielding cunt lips which opened like magic to receive it.

Ivor withdrew and then pushed forward again, this time

completely inserting his throbbing tool inside her tight, clinging sheath. Beth jerked her backside to absorb every inch of his slippery cock and he grunted with satisfaction as he felt himself fully engulfed inside the sweet prison of her juicy cunt. She lifted her hips to welcome his thrusting tool which nestled inside her sopping slit and their bodies moved in a quickening erotic rhythm, faster and faster as Ivor pounded his thick prick in and out of her warm, wet love channel.

Beth raised her legs and locked them around his waist as she panted: 'Lovely, lovely, what a glorious fuck! Come on now, big boy, shoot your load, I want to feel all that creamy jism flooding into me!'

Quite berserk with passion, they swung from side to side as Ivor's tingling cock slewed joyously in and out of Beth's clinging crack. 'There I go!' she squealed and Ivor tensed his frame as with a hoarse cry he crashed down one last time upon Beth's soft body. She screamed her delight as she came just as the first spasm of spunk streamed inside her sopping slit. She squeezed her thighs together and milked every last drop of sticky seed from his spurting shaft.

He collapsed upon her, his entire frame bathed in perspiration. But Beth showed no signs of releasing his cock until it started to deflate and only then did she allow him to withdraw from her drenched cunt and roll over to lie next to her, his chest heaving as he recovered from his exertions.

'Whew! What a smashing fuck! Your cock rates a score of, let me see now, eight and a half out of ten,' remarked Beth cheerfully as she sat up and reached out for her gin and tonic.

'I hope that's good,' said Ivor as he leaned over and kissed her nipple.

'Oh yes, very good indeed, although a man I met last month scored nine and a half. It's funny, but since I split up from Roger, I somehow know within five minutes of meeting a man whether or not we're going to make love. Either the magic ingredient's there or it isn't, and I've rarely been disappointed in my choices.'

He nodded his head sagely and asked: 'Well, what is this magic ingredient which arouses you, Beth?'

'It's very difficult to say,' she replied thoughtfully. 'I'm tall so I suppose I prefer tall men because I don't like to feel big in bed. It's certainly more comfortable if our centres of gravity are close together! A tall man is more able to kiss comfortably whilst we're fucking. Yet I must say that although a tall, lean body is a turn-on, this guy Bob Cripps who I met last month is five inches shorter than me. He never mentioned the difference in our heights because it didn't bother him and I found his self-confidence very sexy.'

'Bob Cripps,' said Ivor thoughtfully. 'Now that name rings a bell. Where have I heard it before?'

'Probably at work because Bob's in your business,' she answered. 'He writes commercials for some big advertising agency and he came up here to choose two of my dogs for a TV commercial.'

'Oh yes, of course, I know who Bob Cripps is. He's a director of Clayton, McCallum, one of these new hot shot agencies which is giving the Saatchi boys a run for their money. I hope to hell they haven't won a dog food account because if they ever worked for my client, I'd lose the work. They have their own in-house public relations department.'

Beth ran her hand across his chest and said soothingly: 'You don't have to worry, this commercial was for a new chocolate bar.'

'Thank goodness for that, we've enough agencies trying to pinch our accounts,' said Ivor with great relief. 'I tell you, love, it's hard enough to grab any new accounts these days and even once you've won them you have to spend half your time fighting off the bloody competition. And if Bob Cripps scored more than nine and a half, it's just as well that he's not working against me.'

Beth tut-tutted her disapproval as she tweaked his nose. 'Now, now, you mustn't be so defeatist, we've still enough time for you to show that you can do as well if not better.' She looked down at his limp prick which lay over his thigh and added: 'Shall I tell you how Bob got me going? That'll get us both in the mood for another screw.'

She leaned over on her side and clasped his flaccid cock in her hand as she began: 'Bob came over to my place with the actors and the film crew to shoot part of this commercial. The idea was to show this couple walking with the dogs who would beg for a piece of chocolate when they stopped to rest. He and the director chose the dogs but then the weather clouded over and as the forecast was for rain later in the day they decided to start shooting first thing the next day.

'The rest of the party went back to Glasgow but Bob asked me if he could stay and take me out to lunch. I was delighted to say yes because he had that magic ingredient – like you do, Ivor, remember, so you don't have to be jealous! I hadn't had sex for about two months and I was more than ready to be seduced by a nice chap like Bob. I grant you he is good-looking but as they say: "men look for beautiful women and women look for interesting men". I was taken by Bob's self-confidence and the amount of interest that he obviously showed in me. I could feel the strength and authority that exuded from him.

'To be honest, I should also admit that I could see the slight bulge in his crotch which also whet my appetite! Anyhow, I sat him down in the living room whilst I changed into a sexy black dress. As my little secret I wore a pair of crotchless panties and I dabbed on some expensive perfume all round my pussy which I hoped Bob would be inhaling after our meal!

'When I went back to the living room he stood up and said: "I hope you don't mind but I've booked a table at Goldstone's." Now that's a very posh restaurant about three miles away and I looked at him and said that he needn't have chosen such an expensive restaurant. "Oh come on, it's my pleasure," he insisted. "I've already booked a taxi and it'll be here in ten minutes."

'I protested that we could have taken my car but he would have none of it. "If we do that you wouldn't be able to enjoy wine with your lunch," he said. I later found out that he was very strict about never driving and drinking since a friend of his was badly injured by a drunken driver seven years ago.'

Ivor muttered: 'Well, one can't argue with the principle but I'll lay odds that the taxi *and* the lunch were stuck on his expenses afterwards.'

Beth pulled his cock and scolded him. 'Don't be cynical now, Ivor, and besides, it didn't alter the fact that I'd already decided that I wanted Bob to fuck me. So off we went in the taxi and we had a wonderful meal and if you have the time, Ivor, you must go to Goldstone's, it's just off the Edinburgh road a mile or two past Forrestfield. We enjoyed a lovely meal, lettuce and almond salad, two superb Scotch beef fillet steaks with pommes frites, washed down with a bottle of very good claret, soft and well berried. By the time Mrs Goldstone put the dessert menu in front of us, I was so full that I couldn't even manage her home-made apricot ice-cream. Bob and I decided to finish off simply with coffee.

'My only excuse for what happened then was that when she served our coffee, Mrs Goldstone insisted on bringing us large brandies with the compliments of the house. They say brandy makes you randy and perhaps it was the liqueur which made me slip off my shoes and move one of my feet up his leg. Bob's eyes widened as he felt my toes wriggle against his stiffening cock but he soon began to grind his groin against them.

'All was calm above the table except for the steamy glance he shot me. When Mrs Goldstone came over to pour us some more coffee, no-one would ever have guessed that his prick was threatening to burst out of his trousers. Some men might have been flustered by what I was doing but Bob gave me a taste of my own medicine! He was wearing slip-ons, making it easy for him also to remove a shoe. Now it was my turn to feel a foot insinuate itself between my legs and move upwards to my crotch. His toes were soon rubbing around my pussy and both of us now were so highly aroused that we could hardly wait to finish our meal and get back to my place and fuck ourselves silly.

'We were so highly charged that we could hardly contain ourselves in the taxi. I was already moist between my legs and perhaps Bob inhaled a trace of my pussy odour as we sat pressed together and he cupped my hip and started a slow, sensual massage of my thigh. He slipped his hand under my dress and I spread my legs for him which caused my short skirt to hike up even further, showing the tops of my stockings. I was sitting on the left hand side of the car against the door, fortunately out of range of the driver's mirror because when Bob discovered that my panties were crotchless, he murmured his appreciation whilst his fingers lightly caressed their way directly through the hole to my pussy bush. When he touched the edges of my cunny, my pussy muscles spasmed and I pushed against his hand to increase the pleasure he was giving me.

'The exciting tingling feeling between my legs was getting stronger and stronger and I gasped out loud when Bob slid one and then two fingers inside my wet slit, probing deep inside me and finding that incredibly sensitive spot which made me shudder violently. In fact I had to bite my fingers to muffle my moans as he stroked and stroked inside my cunny until I thought I would go out of my mind.

'I whimpered uncontrollably as he finger-fucked me, using his thumb to massage my clitty. The seat of the car became damp with my juices as he jabbed his fingers in and out of my honeypot. God knows what the driver would have done if he could have seen my legs spread wide and my hips jerking up and down, pushing against Bob's hand, but I wouldn't have cared. I couldn't have stopped even if I'd have wanted to.

'When we arrived at my front door, we shot out and Bob stuffed a ten shilling note into the driver's hand and waved away the proffered change. Once we were inside I pulled him into the bedroom, took off my dress, removed my soaked panties and spread my legs. Bob looked down at my pouting pussy lips and tore off his clothes in a flash, exposing his throbbing thick tool to my eyes which made my pussy tingle even more. Then he threw himself on top of me and I was so wet that there was no stopping his first thrust as it shot all the way up me, making us both gasp with intense pleasure. Slowly he drew his shaft out again so that just the tip of his knob was inside my cunny and then he pushed his way back in. Oh, this feeling was so glorious! Never in my life had I imagined I could be so full of cock. I was out of this world as he moved this wonderful prick from side to side and round and round inside me.

'The sensations in my cunt were driving me crazy and I came again and again, coating Bob's cock with love juice. He was fucking me so beautifully that my legs flew up in the air as he sank his shaft to depths I didn't know existed. I clung to him, clawing at his back and his firm, round buttocks which were rising and falling over me.

'Then I really exploded and screamed out with happiness, bucking my hips and carrying him high off the bed. I nearly fainted as he drove in even deeper and I felt his fountain of jism splatter inside me as my cunny walls spasmed around his twitching tool. Bob stayed on top of me, being careful to keep his quivering cock in place as we slowly came down from the heights and then he rolled over to my side and we lay panting as we recovered from this marvellous fuck.'

Beth paused and she looked across to Ivor and with a twinkle in her eye she warned: 'Just thinking about Bob's wonderful cock is making me randy again.' She pushed him on to his back and rubbed his hard, swollen shaft with both her hands. Ivor writhed in ecstasy as her silky hair brushed against his prick. She transferred her hands to his heavy, hanging balls as she washed his uncapped purple helmet with her tongue before taking it between her lips and nibbling delicately on the rounded crown.

'Hold on a sec,' said Ivor and he reached out for Beth's unfinished gin and tonic and poured it all over his blue-veined stiffstander. 'That'll make it taste even nicer.'

She smiled and parted her full lips as she took his taut tool into her mouth, bobbing her head up and down. Ivor placed his hands on her head as Beth sucked lustily on his gin-drenched cock and squeezed his balls lightly in one hand. Then she started to frig herself with the fingers of her other hand at the same time. The sight of her fingers flashing in and out of her thick curly bush excited Ivor so much that he was worried that he would ejaculate before he could lie back and enjoy the delicious sensations of being fellated so sensuously.

Beth licked all along his shaft with her delicate tongue, slipping her finger up inside her mouth to tickle his knob whilst her lips slithered up and down his rock-hard boner, letting her tongue swirl over his purple helmet each time he thrust forwards. She sensed that he was about to shoot so she gave his cock a wicked final flick and then lay back on the bed and massaged her pink pussy lips which jutted through the curly hairs which covered her mound. Ivor turned over her and sank his rigid rod into the luscious wet softness and immediately Beth clamped her legs around him so that the walls of her love channel continued to massage his shaft as he pumped madly to and fro, sliding deeper and deeper until he was grinding his knob against her erect clitty.

'God, I'm coming, I'm coming,' she panted and as he knew that his own climax was very near, Ivor pressed his forefinger against her clitty, holding his prick steady inside her as the first electric shocks of orgasm crackled through her soft body. Her hands gripped his bum cheeks and Ivor pistoned his prick in and out of her cunt. Seconds later his torso stiffened as his cock spurted out a fountain of frothy white jism, deluging her cunt with waves of sticky sperm. They sighed in mutual delight at every gush as their love juices mingled together and dribbled down Beth's thighs.

They lay sated for a while and Ivor would have dearly loved to stay in bed with Beth for another hour but it occurred to him that Brian Lipman might return early from Argyll Street and Eddie Taylor could possibly be in need of a helping hand.

'Duty calls, Beth,' he said reluctantly. 'I must get dressed and make sure everything is well with all our friends.'

She looked a little disappointed but she gave him a quick kiss on the cheek. 'It's all right, Ivor, I quite understand, but would you mind very much if I joined you later? I think I've still time to have a nice refreshing bath, if that's okay with you.'

'Of course it is! Stay as long as you like,' said Ivor as he pulled on his pants. He could not help letting a brief smile flit across his face as it struck him that this was the second time today that he had left a girl to recover in his room after he had fucked her. This reminded him that Chrissie, the girl who he had left to breakfast in his bed, would be coming back to the hotel after she finished work. He made a mental note to sort out his evening arrangements, which were becoming slightly complicated because he also wanted to fit in another session with Maggie and Ruth at some stage.

He went downstairs and asked at reception if there were any messages for him. 'Oh yes, there's just one,' said the girl behind the desk. 'A Mr Taylor was here about five minutes ago and said that if you asked for him, he would be in the lounge.'

Ivor gave a small wave of thanks and made his way to the lounge where Eddie Taylor was sitting alone. 'Hello, Eddie, everything going to plan?' asked Ivor. As he plumped down in an armchair next to him, he noticed that Eddie looked a trifle dishevelled, with his collar rumpled and his tie hanging loose and slightly off centre. For a moment he looked anxiously at his client but then Eddie turned his face towards him and let a broad smile crease a path across his face. 'Aye, you could say that,' he said slowly. He leaned across to Ivor and nudged him with his elbow and quietly added: 'Thanks to you, I've had a wonderful afternoon! I'm damned sure Giles Horrobin won't grumble about the hospitality that we've extended to him. Jesus, that man can fuck like a rattlesnake! Frankly, I couldn't keep up with him so I've just left him in the bedroom with the girls.'

'Then you both struck lucky,' commented Ivor with relief and satisfaction in his voice. 'I certainly can't grumble either so, if Brian Lipman hit the jackpot, a good time will have been had by all.'

'Well, good luck to him and I hope he enjoys himself as much as I did. Vicky and Suzie were tremendous, Ivor, you'll hardly believe what happened. We'd all had some sandwiches at the press conference so we only had a main course for lunch which Giles insisted on paying for. Then Vicky said: "Did you know that the Scottish tennis championships are on television this afternoon? I'd love to watch a game or two if we could find a set somewhere. We've well over an hour before Maggie and Ruth come back with the photographer."

'Giles looked at me and said: "Eddie, your room has a television, doesn't it? Would you mind if Vicky and I watched the tennis there?"

'"By all means," I said but then Suzie chipped in: "I've got an even better idea. Why don't Eddie and I go upstairs with you?" Giles looked at her darkly but his face cleared when she said sweetly? "Don't worry, we won't cramp your style."

'Well, I wasn't too sure what to say but Vicky agreed with her friend and said: "Good idea, Suze, I always prefer playing doubles rather than singles."

'"So do I," giggled Suzie as Giles signalled a waiter to

bring the bill. "I even prefer a foursome at tennis!" But even then I didn't really guess what the girls had in store for us. Well, as I said, Giles paid the bill and we marched up to the room you had reserved for me. The girls looked stunning in their hot pants and I was already getting excited. I guessed there might be a chance of some rumpy-pumpy although, to be honest with you, I didn't know exactly how far the girls would go.

'I switched on and we set about making ourselves comfortable. Giles and I took off our jackets and then he and Vicky sprawled themselves out on the bed whilst I sat down in an armchair. Suzie sat on the floor between my legs, with her head leaning back against my groin. I don't think we'd watched the tennis for more than ten minutes before I turned my head and saw Giles and Vicky in a clinch. His hand was caressing her breasts and she was rubbing the big bulge in his pants with the palm of her hand. Suzie had seen what was happening and she teased me by pressing her head against my prick, which was already stiffening up as I saw Giles squeeze Vicky's gorgeous bosom.

'Vicky noticed us looking at her and she said: "Okay folks, shall I order some coffee from room service or can you all wait for a minute whilst I finish off Giles's cock?"

'Suzie and I laughed but Giles was a bit indignant and said: "It'll take more than a minute to finish me off, my girl!"

'"Oh yeah? No man ever lasts more than sixty seconds of my sucking," she said. She let her hand trace the outline of Giles's boner on the outside of his trousers as she added approvingly: "Goodness me, Mr Horrobin, what a whopper. But the bigger they are, the harder they fall!"

'Suzie swung round and knelt before me. As she

fondled my own stiff tool she said in a husky voice: "I bet I can bring Eddie off before you can make Giles spunk."

'"Is that a challenge?" asked Vicky with a gleam in her eye. I saw Giles's face flush as Suzie replied with a lewd giggle: "Sure, we'll make a contest of it. We'll start together and pull back when they come so there can be no argument."

'Vicky nodded and unbuckled Giles's belt whilst Suzie unzipped my flies. "Hold on a minute, girls, this isn't fair," Giles protested. "You're getting to suck our cocks but we aren't getting to see any of you."

'"Oh, but if we undress, you'll come even quicker," said Vicky as her fingers delved skilfully into Giles's trousers.

'"Well at least go topless for us," I said, my voice shaking as Vicky brought out Giles's prick. She showed that she hadn't been simply flattering him about the size of his wedding tackle – he had an enormous chopper, at least nine inches long and probably even thicker than mine and I'm quite well endowed. Perhaps it was the sight of his colossal cock which made Vicky say: "What the hell, let's all strip off."

'It didn't take long for us to agree and once we were naked, Suzie knelt in front of my legs with one hand gripping my straining shaft and the other cupping my balls. Vicky was grasping Giles's gigantic cock in the same way and she said: "Are you ready, Suze? One, two, three, *go!*"

'I closed my eyes as I felt the first touch of Suzie's wet lips on my prick. Then I opened them and looked down on her pretty head bobbing up and down as she washed my shaft with saliva. Then I glanced across to the bed and saw Giles's gigantic helmet disappear into Vicky's mouth. This sight coupled with Suzie's sucking drove me wild, especially when Suzie began to wank me off whilst she gobbled on my knob and I started to moan as I felt the spunk shooting up from my balls. "I win!" cried out Suzie as a fountain of spunk spurted out of my cock but Vicky was too busy sliding her lips up and down Giles's huge penis to notice. Suzie held my twitching tool in her hand as she licked up the sticky seed. When she was finished, she scrambled up to sit on my lap and we watched Vicky finish Giles off.

'We saw her open her mouth as wide as she could and somehow she managed to stuff almost all of his massive truncheon into her mouth. His knob must have been almost touching the back of her throat as she sucked and slurped on this large lollipop. Then we noticed her begin swallowing in anticipation as she squeezed his balls. Sure enough, almost immediately her mouth was filled with his cum but as Suzie had already won the bet, she didn't bother to pull back. She gulped down all Giles's jism, letting his cock out of her mouth so that she could tongue his helmet until, at last, his shaft started to soften. She moved her head away and sat up next to him.

'"Yes, you've won, Suzie," she agreed. "It's just as well we didn't have a bet on it, but I think you're still entitled to a prize. Is there anything you'd particularly like?"

'"I'd rather like to be fucked by that tremendous tadger you've been sucking," she replied brightly. She turned to me and said: "No offence, Eddie, and you're welcome to have me later, but I've never seen a prick quite as big as Giles's. I've a fancy to see if I can cram it in my pussy."

'Giles cleared his throat and said: "You're more than welcome, as far as I'm concerned, but I need to have a rest between the rounds these days. When I was seventeen I could keep screwing even after I'd come, but now I have to take a break after I've spunked."

'"Well, quality's far more important than quantity," said Suzie as she lifted herself off me. As she went across to snuggle up to her friend on the bed, she went on: "Anyhow, it'll give Vicky and I a chance to enjoy each other." With this she kissed Vicky's ear-lobe and probably more for the benefit of Giles and me she said: "Watch me suck Vicky's pouting pussy lips. I'm going to slide my tongue all along her juicy crack and make her pussy tingle and throb whilst I nip on her clitty."'

Eddie paused and wiped his brow as Ivor commented: 'Quite a girl, that Suzie. She didn't talk as much as the others, but I've often found out that once the quiet girls get going, there's no stopping them.'

'Well, that was sure true of Suzie, though Vicky didn't need any persuading to join in the fun and games! She just lay back and sighed whilst Suzie climbed on top of her and immediately began to tweak her big strawberry nipples between her fingers and daintily manipulate them up to hard little red bullets. They exchanged a fiery French kiss until Suzie withdrew and slid her mouth first to one nipple and then the other and then across Vicky's quivering belly and down to the silky thatch of black curls between her thighs. Vicky swung her legs over Suzie's back and rested her feet on the ripe white globes of her bottom.

'I don't know about Giles, but my own cock began to stiffen as I watched Suzie lick along the edges of Vicky's crack and then gently slide her hand around her slit, obviously enjoying the soft rub of Vicky's pussy hair. Suzie dipped a finger between her soft, yielding pink pussy lips and Vicky murmured: "Oooh, that's gorgeous, really gorgeous," as Suzie began to finger-fuck the trembling girl, pressing her thumb and forefinger together as she plunged them in and out of Vicky's juicy cunny.

68

'"Oooh, look, your clitty's popped out," said Suzie. I craned my neck for a quick look before Suzie swooped down and sucked it into her mouth. She pressed her lips firmly against Vicky's quim and began to lick and lap at her squelchy snatch.

'A strangled cry from Giles made me look up. I saw him swing himself behind Suzie and pull away Vicky's feet from Suzie's arse. He slicked his hand up and down his huge prick, which had now recovered from Vicky's plating and was standing up high against his belly. She saucily stuck out her bumcheeks and reached back to guide Giles's monster member into her cunt, fearing perhaps that he might attempt to bum-fuck her with his oversized tool. However, Giles was more than happy simply to fuck Suzie doggie-style. He splayed open her lovely bum cheeks to make a wider crevice for his cock. Once he was inside her, they began to rock to and fro as Giles slid his hand round to her pussy to diddle her clit whilst he fucked her.

'By now my prick was bursting and so I jumped up on the bed next to them and offered my cock to Vicky who, without hesitation, grabbed hold of it and pulled my knob towards her mouth. She opened her lips and swirled her wet tongue around my knob before beginning to suck vigorously on my shaft. I rolled my hips back and forth as she gobbled my tadger whilst Suzie continued to lick out her pussy. Then suddenly Vicky clasped my cock and drummed her legs wildly on the mattress and I guessed that she was about to come. However, she didn't stop sucking my cock with long, slurping strokes as she threshed her body from side to side. When she shivered all over with the force of her climax, she brought up her other hand to squeeze my dangling ballsack. This made me spend straightaway and I shot my load down her throat which she gulped down whilst at the same time Giles creamed Suzie's cunny with a coating of hot spunk.

'Well now, despite his earlier protestations about not being as virile as he was when he was a lad, Giles was ready for more fucking! He lay on his back with Suzie on one side and Vicky on the other and they took it in turns to wank his big stiffie which was sticking up like a veiny flagpole between his legs. They bent their faces forward and licked his prick, one from the left and the other from the right. They cradled their hands round his balls as they tongued his knob together.

'I'll be honest, I'd have loved to have carried on. Tell me if I'm wrong, Ivor, I don't believe there can be many men who possess such staying power. But I'm not a spoilsport so I slipped off the bed, dressed myself and left them to it.'

'Very decent of you,' said Ivor with an amused smile.

Eddie shrugged his shoulders. 'Well, remember that the whole gang bang was for Giles's benefit anyway, and I wasn't missed. As I left I saw that Suzie was squatting over his mouth so that he could lick her out whilst Vicky was bouncing up and down on his wiggling shaft.'

Ivor waved at a passing waiter and asked Eddie if he wanted a drink. After ordering two large whiskies, Ivor commented: 'This Mr Horrobin sounds like quite a sexual athlete. Does he have a reputation as a ladies' man?'

'No, and I wouldn't spread it about the trade that he's such a great cocksman,' said Eddie as he straightened his tie. 'I don't want any of our competitors getting to know how they can best interest him. I'd like to keep this particular marketing ploy to ourselves. And talking of keeping things to ourselves, I was just wondering where Beth could be found. Just between the two of us, would I be right in thinking that she could be found in your bedroom?'

Ivor raised his hands in mock surrender and said: 'All our dealings with clients and suppliers are strictly confidential, Eddie, but I wouldn't deny it. Please don't tell anyone though, it wouldn't be right.'

'I won't say a word,' Eddie promised as the waiter brought them their drinks. 'Oh look, isn't that Brian Lipman with his two girls over there?'

'Yes, you could hardly miss Maggie and Ruth in those costumes,' said Ivor and the two men stood up as their colleagues spotted them and made their way over to the table where the waiter was still hovering.

'Hi, everyone,' said the photographer genially as he pulled up a chair. 'It's all right for some, downing Scotch all afternoon whilst the girls and I work our butts off. Never mind, I'm sure there's plenty more in the bottle. What's your poison, girls, Ivor's buying.'

The girls plumped themselves down on a small sofa and considered the question. 'I'd like a Glenmorangie, please,' said Ruth. Maggie nodded her head. 'I'll have the same,' she said and Brian told the waiter to make it three. 'I don't know what we're drinking,' he confessed, 'but when in Rome, do as the Romans do. What is this Glenmorangie when it's at home?'

'It's one of the best single malt whiskies,' explained Eddie Taylor. 'You're used to blended scotch, Brian, but you're in for a treat if you've never tried a single malt before.'

'Well whilst you're waiting, tell us how it all went – did you give away all the coupons, girls? Hey, wait a minute though, where are the dogs?'

'Oh, don't worry,' said Ruth as she slipped off her shoe and caressed her foot. 'All that walking about has made my feet sore. Ivor, may I have a bath in your room before we go?'

'Yes, yes, of course, but what about the dogs?' repeated Ivor, dreading the thought of having to break any bad news to Beth Rokeby.

But Maggie assured him that his concern was unfounded. 'Oh, they're back at the kennels,' she said. 'My boy friend Ken, who's Beth's brother, came along to take some photographs for the *Evening Express* and as it was his last job for the day, he volunteered to take them back to his sister's place. Wasn't that kind of him?'

'Yeah, it's saved us all a bother as we're all getting a bit pushed for time,' said Brian, dumping his bag to the ground. 'After we've had a quick drink, girls, I'll take those photos that you wanted.'

'Oh thanks, Brian, we're in desperate need of some new shots for our portfolios,' said Ruth. As she looked round she saw Beth Rokeby walking towards the group and called out: 'Hiya, Beth, we're over here.'

Ivor pre-empted Beth's question when she approached them by telling her immediately that by courtesy of her brother, the dogs were all safely back home in their kennels. 'Thanks for telling me, Ivor,' she said as the waiter brought their drinks. 'I guessed that might happen. Ken did mention at the press conference that he might be able to take them back for me.'

'What will you have, Beth?' invited Eddie but as she sat down next to Maggie and Ruth she said: 'No thank you, Eddie, my brother's invited me to a party tonight which a gang of journalists are giving for Steve Elsey, one of his colleagues on the *Express*. He's leaving Glasgow next week for a job on the *Daily Mirror* photo-desk in Manchester. I reckon it'll be a pretty wild affair so I'd best keep off the booze till then.

'And that reminds me, everyone, Ken's asked me to say that you're all be very welcome to come to this shindig.

It's at a flat in Renfrew Street just behind the dental hospital which isn't too far away. Ken says the party won't start until half past nine when the first editions of the morning papers have come out and I don't think it will really get going till nearer midnight. So if you're already fixed up for this evening, come along later.'

'Oh yes, you must all come!' said Maggie with enthusiasm. She pointed a finger at Ivor and added: 'Ken told me about it a few days ago and it could be very worthwhile for you, as you'll be able to meet a lot of the top Scottish journalists who'll be rolling up to say good-bye to Steve.'

The waiter came back and set down three large Glenmorangie whiskies on the table by Brian Lipman. He handed two of the glasses to Maggie and Ruth and then picked up his own glass and inspected the clear liquid inside it.

'A single malt whisky should be savoured rather than just chucked down the throat,' counselled Eddie Taylor and Brian sensibly heeded this wise advice. He sipped delicately at his drink and then smacked his lips. 'M'mm, I see what you mean, it's nice, very nice, smooth tasting but with a real bite to it.'

But Brian had little time to relax because Ruth and Maggie soon reminded him of his promise to take some photographs of them. 'No peace for the wicked,' he sighed as he picked up his equipment. 'Bye bye for now, everybody. Beth, perhaps we'll see each other later at this party. I'd like to pop in for an hour or so later on.'

'Good, I hope you two will also make an appearance,' said Maggie to Ivor and Eddie. 'But if we don't see you there, thanks for the job, we've enjoyed it, haven't we, Ruthie?'

'Yes, it's been fun,' agreed Ruth. 'Your dogs were very docile, Beth. I was holding Honey when a couple of toddlers came close and were playing with her and she stood patiently whilst they pulled her ears. She didn't bat an eyelid.'

'Honey wouldn't snap unless she was really put upon,' said Beth with satisfaction. 'Bitches are usually more easy-going but in fact the majority of dogs can be trained not to be anti-social. You just have to have the patience to teach them how to behave with people.'

'It's not always so easy,' commented Eddie. 'My girl friend has a very lovable cocker spaniel and although Rexie's house-trained, he doesn't seem to take much notice when she tells him off.'

'Well, it could be that she's giving him the wrong signals,' she said as Eddie and the girls left the group for what was to prove a very interesting photo-session. 'You must always be aware of what your face is saying. Dog facial expressions carry specific meanings and so, to them, do ours. For instance, a wildly happy dog can't keep its mouth shut any more than we can when we're bursting with joy.

'But you mustn't laugh during training because a dog knows what a laugh is all about – fun! – and with that all attempts at discipline break down. Like wolves, dogs need a respected, powerful leader, so tell your girl friend that the next time Rexie misbehaves, she should show her authority just as the head of a wolf pack shows his dominance by glowering and snarling at anyone who steps out of line. The best way to scold your dog is to stand over him and stare hard. If he's still not paying attention, bare your teeth and try to snarl out the words. And a shake of the finger makes a good substitute for the pack leader's snapping gesture.'

Ivor remarked: 'You have to show him that you're the boss, just like a parent has to do with a kiddie.'

'Exactly, and a good way to reinforce your status is to grasp the muzzle of your dog in your hand and shake it gently like a dominant wolf will take a junior's muzzle in its jaws. The response will be a big lick. I'm sorry to tell you that the reason why dogs lick isn't simply affection, a sort of doggy kiss, but a restatement of their acceptance of you as their mentor.'

Beth rummaged in her bag and gave Eddie her business card. 'Do call me if you would like to bring your girl friend and her dog over to my place,' she said. 'I'll gladly take you through some training exercises for Rexie.

'Now I must be on my way though I do hope you'll both come to this press party tonight. Hold on, let me scribble the address on the back of my card. As I said, it won't liven up till late and I dare say that you'll be even more welcome if you bring a bottle.'

'I'll be there at around eleven o'clock,' said Ivor promptly. 'It'll give me a great opportunity to meet some important Scottish journalists. What about you, Eddie? Would you like to meet me here and we'll go together?'

He shook his head. 'No, I'm afraid I'll have to pass as I have some paperwork I must catch up on this evening, but thanks again for the invite. Beth, it's been awfully nice meeting you and I hope we'll be able to use your dogs again for promotion work. Give me another card and I'll give Ivor this one, it's got the address of the party on the back.'

Beth shook hands with both men and was walking away to the door when Ivor suddenly remembered that he had left her the key of his room. 'Excuse me a minute, Eddie,' he muttered and he followed her outside into the lobby.

He caught her sleeve as she reached the reception desk and Beth winked at him and said: 'I know what you want, Ivor, don't worry, I was just about to hand in your key. Look, will you really turn up at the party?'

'Sure, I'll be there all right, and not only to make some more contacts,' he pledged. 'It's because I'd love to see you again. The only snag is that Brian and I have already made arrangements for tonight and so we might not be able to come by ourselves.'

Ivor looked at her apologetically. 'In other words you've already made dinner dates with Vicky and Suzie,' she said with evident disappointment in her voice. 'Well, you bring them along, I'm sure they'd enjoy themselves.'

'No, you're wrong, Brian and I aren't having dinner with Vicky and Suzie – I wouldn't mind so much if we were,' said Ivor shamelessly. 'In fact we have to entertain a couple of people from Websters, the supermarket chain which Eddie needs to get behind the Four Seasons launch.' His explanation which was not exactly a fib was at best somewhat economical with the truth.

'Oh, so it's a business dinner then,' said Beth and Ivor nodded, being only too pleased to leave her thinking that he and Brian were spending the evening on duty with two supermarket executives.

'What can I do?' said Ivor, shrugging his shoulders. 'International Pet Products is one of our biggest clients and if necessary, I have to make myself available twenty-four hours a day. But never fear, I'll see you later at the party, that's a promise.'

Beth smiled her pleasure as she gave him back the key of his bedroom. 'Good, I'll see you later then,' she said and then in a whisper, she added: 'Perhaps we can come back here afterwards and start again from where we left off this afternoon.'

'I'd love to say yes,' said Ivor cautiously, 'but I'd better not promise in case the night staff here are a bit fussy. You know how stuffy these hotels can be though, come to think of it, my booking is for a double room.'

He kissed Beth on the cheek and said: 'Bye for now,' before walking back briskly to the lounge where he saw that Eddie had been joined by Vicky and Suzie. They both looked rather exhausted after their protracted sex session with Giles Horrobin. 'Hello there, you two okay? Where's our marathon man got to?' Ivor asked. Suzie lifted her arm and flapped her wrist limply towards the exit. 'He's left, Ivor, he went straight down in the lift to the car park but as I just mentioned to Eddie, he asked us to thank you both again for a great presentation.'

Vicky sighed deeply and said: 'He's a nice guy and what a gigantic cock he had! Yes, he's hung like a donkey but do you know, if anything it's a bit too big for me. I don't know about you, Suzie, but I don't think I could take such an enormous shaft every night.'

'Oh, I don't know, I didn't have any problems,' said Suzie cheerfully. 'Still, as the Yanks say, it's not the size of the ship that counts, it's the motion of the ocean.

'But your prick was just as nice as his jumbo-sized tool,' she said hastily to Eddie. 'Now never mind about Giles, where did you say you were taking Vicky and me to dinner this evening?'

Oh ho, so that's why you don't want to come to the party tonight, Mr Taylor, said Ivor to himself. He looked on with amusement at the crimson flush which had appeared on Eddie's face as he replied: 'I thought we might go to Goldstone's. Have either of you ever been there? It's only a mile or so past Forrestfield and it'll be a nice night for a drive out of town.'

Suzie had never sampled the delights of Tricia

Goldstone's kitchen but Vicky said enthusiastically: 'Smashing! Ken took me there once last summer and we had a delicious meal. You'll love it, Suzie, I know you will.'

'Sounds super, and I just wish that I could join you,' said Ivor. He recalled that Beth had told him earlier about the restaurant. 'Eddie, would you excuse me, but I think I'd better touch base with Brian Lipman.'

'By all means, Ivor, for heaven's sake let's call it a day. I suggest that we rendezvous back here at twelve o'clock tomorrow and see if we've made any of the papers.'

'Fine, Eddie, I'll see you tomorrow,' Ivor replied. 'Remember, we've also put our press cuttings service on stand-by to monitor all the radio and TV shows so by noon the office will have called me to let me know how we've fared.

'Now, Vicky and Suzie,' he went on, spreading out his hands. 'Girls, what can I say? You've both done a marvellous job and I certainly hope we'll be able to work together again in Glasgow. Meanwhile, if either of you are ever in London, I'll take it as a personal affront if you don't give me a ring and let me take you out for a drink.'

Ivor gave them a good-bye kiss, shook hands with Eddie Taylor and decided to go back to his room. He had to ring Martin Reece back at Cable's offices in London and reassure him that the first phase of the Four Seasons launch had got off to a flying start.

He unlocked his room and was glad to see that the clothes which Maggie and Ruth had left there when they changed into their Four Seasons costumes had disappeared. Ivor correctly surmised that the girls had taken their belongings across the corridor to Brian Lipman's room. He put in a call to his office and lay down on the bed and relaxed, his hands behind his head, whilst the operator made the connection. He wondered how he should plan his evening.

He smiled wryly as he realised that he was caught in possession of an *embarrass de riches*. Chrissie, the gorgeous blonde he had slept with the previous night, was expecting to have dinner with him tonight and her friend Paula had made a similar date with Brian Lipman. He and Brian could cancel the arrangements but even discounting the fact that it would be a rotten thing to do, it might not be too smart a move to upset the girls. They both worked at Websters' supermarket in Argyll Street and it would be foolish to take even the slightest chance of damaging the Four Seasons promotion at the group's flagship store in the heart of Glasgow.

Furthermore, he had to consider the little matter of Chrissie's brother-in-law who might hold the key to a new account – so standing up the girls this evening was out. On the other hand, how the dickens could he take Chrissie to the party? She would be furious if he paid court to Beth Rokeby, who in turn would hardly be happy to find out that the grocery trade pet foods buyer, with whom Ivor had supposedly talked business with over dinner, was none other than the sensuous blonde bombshell hanging on his arm! Still, it would be the lesser of two evils although any hopes of ever spending the night again with Beth would be lost for good.

'You can't win them all,' he said to the telephone which answered with a ring and Ivor picked up the receiver. 'Hello, Cable Publicity? Hello, Jilly, it's Ivor Belling here. I'm calling from Glasgow. Is Martin Reece still in the office? Yes? I'd like a quick word with him please.

'Martin: Hi, how are you? Yup, so far everything's gone tickety boo. The press and the trade people all turned up and Eddie Taylor's very pleased with what we've done.'

Ivor heard Martin purr with satisfaction but then he passed on the news about Jeff Mountjoy leaving International Pet Products and how Eddie Taylor was in line for the position of product manager – a job which carried with it the responsibility of choosing the public relations agency to help promote Four Seasons and the group's other dog foods.

He could almost hear his chairman grind his teeth as Martin let vent to his angry frustration. 'Fuck it, that's all we need, just three weeks before we're supposed to present IPP with our publicity plans for the next twelve months. Christ, I'd like to stick a tin of Four Seasons up Jeff Mountjoy's arse. The bastard never mentioned it to me when I took him to the Hunkiedorie Club last week. The least he could have done was to let me know there were changes in the wind. Of course you realise that young Nick Clee will throw his hat in the ring?'

'Yes, and I know that his uncle is a director of Baum and Whitaker PR so it's vital that Eddie steps into Jeff's shoes,' said Ivor grimly.

'Well, that's it, then, Ivor,' said Martin with a note of finality in his voice. 'We'll live or die by the success or otherwise of Four Seasons up in Bonnie Scotland. If it sells well in both test markets then we'll have a national launch with Eddie Taylor in the chair. But even if the stuff doesn't do well in the other test market, and they decide against a national launch, we're still in with a chance. If Eddie shows that he can sell where others can't, he'll walk into Jeff's job and we'll still be flavour of the month.

'So it's all down to you, Ivor, old son. We desperately need a result – a good set of sell-in sales from Eddie and some good press clippings to help the sell-out. For what it's worth I've seen the TV ads which start running on Friday and they should help clear the tins from the shelves. Tell me, do you think it's worth staying an extra couple of days to see if there's anything more we could do?'

Ivor considered the proposition and replied: 'I was going to suggest that myself, Martin. I'm meeting a clutch of top media people at a big party tonight and it could be worthwhile hanging on to see if I can squeeze any more mileage out of the launch whilst I'm up here. Oh yes, and there's also the possibility of snapping up a new account which I want to follow up.' He explained to Martin how he found out that the Edinburgh-based Jetstream Showers were on the look-out for a London publicity agency.

'Their managing director is off to London soon to see some agency presentations but we'd have a head start if he felt that someone had taken the trouble to shoot up to Scotland to fully research the business before showing off their own marketing ideas.'

'You could have a point there,' mused Martin thought-fully. 'Yes, indeed you could – hey, Ivor, we're in luck. Do you remember all that work Craig Grey did last March for Brenda Stanleigh, those posh interior designers who asked us to pitch for their business?'

'Yes, though I wasn't actually involved, Martin, it was you and Toby Nedas who handled the presentation. We were on the short-list, weren't we but Horne, Garwood pipped us at the post.'

'Right and may they choke on it. Craig spent a nice few bob researching all the facts and figures about bathrooms which I could mail up to you. Hold on though, I can do even better – isn't Saturday the fifteenth? Craig's flying to Edinburgh on Friday to give a talk at this European Market Research Seminar. He's booked in at the North

British hotel for Friday and Saturday nights but I'm sure he could leave a day earlier and fly up to Glasgow tomorrow.'

This was good news indeed, for Craig Grey was Cable's bright young head of research. Having on hand an ally who was already knowledgeable about the market would be very helpful when talking to the Jetstream management. 'Great stuff Martin, I'll book Craig in here for tomorrow night and go on over to Edinburgh with him if necessary. Meanwhile, I'll keep a close watch on the Four Seasons situation. And that reminds me, Brian Lipman's flying back tomorrow morning. Could you make sure that Julie Davies has the trade press releases ready to shoot out? The photos will be ready after lunch and Brian said he'd come in and help Julie with the captions. We must have the prints sent round to Mike Sulsh at *The Grocer* by five o'clock if we want to make the current issue.

''Don't fret, I'll see to everything this end. Best of luck, Ivor, keep in touch. Oh, and as I guessed you'd ring this evening I checked with your office and there's nothing there that can't wait till your return. But just to keep myself *au fait* with what's going on, I'm taking your new secretary Debbie out to dinner at the Hunkiedorie Club tonight.'

'Bloody hell, Martin, Debbie's the best secretary I've had since Sheena Walshaw left us. You promised to keep your mitts off Debbie, because if you begin screwing her she won't stay with us long, they never do.' But the only response from Martin was a deep chuckle as he said: 'Sorry, Ivor, but my dear lady wife is away in Belgium for three days and I didn't force you to hire a pretty nineteen-year-old redhead who wears the shortest miniskirt in the whole office and always wiggles her bum when she walks past me.

'See you soon, old boy. I'll buzz Craig Grey this very minute and ask him to prepare some material for you. 'Bye for now.'

'Cheers, Martin,' said Ivor and he replaced the receiver and lay still for a few moments. Then he swung his legs off the bed and decided to walk across the corridor and knock on Brian Lipman's door. It would make sense to talk over tactics for tonight with Brian before Chrissie and Paula arrived. In any event, he wondered what his randy colleague was getting up to with Maggie and Ruth.

As Ivor approached Brian's bedroom he thought he detected the sounds of giggling which stopped suddenly when he rapped his knuckles on the door. 'Who's that?' called out the photographer. 'It's only me,' Ivor replied. Although he did not hear Brian's reply, he heard the key turn in the door which opened slightly and Ruth's face peeped out.

'Quick, come on in,' she smiled and opened the door just wide enough to let him squeeze through. Ivor was not entirely surprised to see that Ruth was naked as, presumably, were Brian and Maggie who were in bed together. Ruth scuttled back and dived under the sheets whilst Brian heaved himself up to a sitting position with an arm round each of the girls.

'Well, I hope you took some good shots of the girls for their portfolios,' said Ivor a little grumpily. 'What are you doing now, Brian? Waiting for the films to be developed?'

'I wish we could,' he replied. 'But in fact you've come in bang at the right moment. Maggie was just about to tell us about the sexy times she had as a student nurse before she became a model.'

He removed his arm from around her shoulders and pulled down the sheet so that Ivor could see her proud, jutting breasts. 'It's a crying shame you left the Health Service, love, because what you could offer you can't get on prescription!

'Maggie used to be a nurse at the Glasgow Infirmary, Ivor,' Brian explained as he fondled Maggie's elongated tawny nipples. 'I'm sure that her alternative therapy worked wonders! Now what was the story you were about to tell us about the footballer?'

Maggie gave a throaty chuckle and said: 'If you like, though you might think I was rather naughty. Basically, it's how I helped this nice young lad named Iain MacGregor snap out of a bad depression. Iain was a good-looking hunky twenty-one-year-old who had been admitted to casualty one Saturday afternoon with a suspected broken ankle. He'd been playing for Bearsden United in a Scottish Junior Cup match but he'd been carried off and driven straight to the Infirmary. The poor lad was in agony and Dr Giddens had to give him a shot of morphine before I wheeled him downstairs for X rays. As expected, poor Iain had broken his ankle so badly that he needed to have an operation later that evening.

'Now as you can imagine, our surgical registrar, Mr Corney, is used to repairing broken limbs during the football season. Although poor Iain had suffered a very bad break, the repair operation was completely successful. But the next day Mr Corney told him that he'd be in hospital for at least a week, and then he would need to wear a plaster for a further month. "Will I be able to play football again?" asked Iain and Mr Corney said he probably would be as good as new, but that Iain shouldn't even think about kicking a ball around for at least another twelve months.

'I happened to be standing by his bed during Mr Corney's visit and when the surgeon left I noticed how depressed Iain looked. So when I brought him round a cup of tea, I said to him: "Cheer up, it's only a matter of time and you'll be as right as rain once your ankle has healed."

'"Will I?" he said gloomily. "This couldn't have happened at a worse time. A couple of months ago my girl friend and I broke up and even more important, I was supposed to go for a job interview next Thursday."

'"Oh come on now," I said as I pulled up a chair and sat next to him, "As far as your girl friend's concerned, a handsome man like you won't have any problem finding another one. And as for your job, I'm sure they'll understand if you ask for the interview to be postponed for a week or so."

'He shook his head sadly and said: "Thanks for trying to buck me up, nurse. I do miss Sheila, but hopefully, I'll find someone else. I've blown the interview though, no doubt about it. You see, it was for a pretty special job – a new position of sports instructor at Florida State University. I've got my diploma in teaching sport from St Duncan's Academy and I'm sure I only made the short list because I specialise in soccer. It's a fast-growing game in the States and the Americans wanted someone who could coach and also play for the University side. Well, that's now out of the question, of course."

'"But you'll be out of plaster in about a month," I said, trying to console him, but he shook his head again and said: "Maybe so, but you heard what Mr Corney told me. I won't be able to play again for at least a year and the University want someone to go out there in eight weeks' time."

'Poor Iain! His parents and friends came to visit him and they were very concerned about how depressed and withdrawn he had become. On his fourth day in the hospital, he was sitting in a chair whilst I was making his bed and I noticed that he was staring at my breasts. Frankly, I don't think he was even aware of what he was doing but I didn't mind; in fact, I rather enjoyed it. So I gave him as many opportunities to have a closer look as I could and I managed to press my tits against him once or twice.

'The very next day I was on the night shift and by eleven o'clock all was quiet in the ward. My friend Tina was on duty with me and she promised to keep a look-out, though it was unlikely that we would be disturbed. So I went round to Iain's bed and drew the curtain around it. Iain was already half asleep but he soon woke up when I pulled off the sheet and lay down next to him. "I think you need cheering up," I whispered as I kissed him. Sleepy and depressed he may have been, but the passion of his response astounded me. He hungrily sucked my tongue into his mouth which was so warm and moist that I could have stayed glued to it for hours.

'But I had more pressing business in mind, and Iain watched with intent fascination as I unbuttoned my blouse and guided his hands inside it. The lovely boy looked stunned when he realised that I wasn't wearing a bra. He cupped each breast in his hands, exploring the shape and firmness with little squeezes and strokes. I shrugged off the blouse completely and his eyes gleamed at the sight of my smooth bare breasts. He pulled gently on my nipples and I drew closer so that he could lick them as I could draw his stiff, hard cock from out of his boxer shorts. Then very carefully, I straddled him, lifting my skirt. Iain gasped with pleasure when his hand roamed up between my legs and he discovered that I'd already taken off my panty girdle before I went on duty and I was only wearing a garter belt and stockings. His fingers caressed my naked pussy and I wriggled up over him so that my cunny was directly over his face. Then I sat down with Iain's lips pressing against my crack. He pulled my pussy lips apart with his thumbs and gripped my thighs powerfully as he began to lick me out. My whole body trembled as the tip of his tongue flicked against my clitty.

'"Ooooh! How lovely!" I panted as I spread my legs wider and closed my eyes. My head rolled from side to side as I pulled and pinched my nipples. With a long, shattering orgasm, a hundred fireworks exploded between my legs as my love juices came rushing through my love channel and splashed down onto Iain's face.

'I was now more than ready to be fucked. I moved down his body as he tugged his shorts down to the top of his plaster. He reached up to cup my breasts whilst I took hold of his thick, throbbing prick and for a short time I squatted, suspended above him, with the tip of his shining knob just brushing against my pouting pussy lips. Then I eased myself down on his juicy boner and he felt really big inside me as I flung myself up and down on his quivering cock. The plaster didn't prevent Iain from meeting my downward plunges with robust upward thrusts of his own and I gyrated up and down in a lovely ride on his rigid length.

'It would have been grand to have fucked away for longer but I knew that the houseman would soon be making his round so I reached down and squeezed Iain's balls. Leaning forward, I muttered in his ear: "I'm coming, I'm coming and I'm going to pump the sperm out of your cock! Shoot your spunk into my cunt, you big-cocked boy!"

'This did the trick and I took him to the root as I slammed down on his thick shaft. Sobbing with relief, Iain pumped a jet of jism inside me at the very moment I began to climb the heights to another shattering orgasm.

'I heard a murmur of voices and there was just time for me to pull on my blouse and to pull back the sheet on top of Iain before the doctor stuck his head through the curtain and asked me if all was well with my patient.

'"Everything's fine, Doctor Cheetham, I was just making Mr MacGregor a wee bit more comfortable," I explained as I pulled open the curtains round Iain's bed. He looked at me a trifle suspiciously at first and I think he might have guessed what had happened but Doctor Cheetham was in no position to make a fuss. It was well known that he used the Matron's office to shag any nurse whom he could lure inside there!

'Iain recovered his spirits very quickly after this little bout and although he did lose the chance of going on the short list for the job in Florida, he did get to America a few months later and is now working at a health club in San Francisco. We've kept in touch and next year I hope to go out and see him again. So it's a story with a happy ending.'

'It's a pity you ever left nursing, Maggie,' said Brian somewhat indistinctly, as he nuzzled his head between her gorgeous breasts. 'I've always said that a really good fuck's worth all the tonics and pep pills in the chemist's shop. Believe me, you would have saved the Health Service a bloody fortune.'

Ivor sat down on the bed and, pretending to be serious, he said solemnly: 'I don't think a fuck would always be suitable, Brian. For instance, after I had my wisdom teeth out last year, I needed a strong pain-killer and not even a blow job from Kathy Kirby would have helped me!

'But tell me, Maggie, why did you give up nursing? Was it the money?'

She smiled and said: 'In a word – yes! It was Ruthie here who introduced me to modelling and even though the work's erratic, I still earn at least double if not three times what I was getting as a nurse. Now come on, Ivor, take your clothes off and let's be having you!'

He looked at her with a puzzled expression and Ruthie said reproachfully: 'Oh, Ivor, don't you remember? When Maggie and I had changed into the Four Seasons costumes, you promised to fuck us when we came back to the hotel after giving out those coupons.'

Brian Lipman snorted with laughter and said: 'Come on, Mr Belling, a promise is a promise. I'm sure we can find room for one more in this bed, so strip off and let's be having you.'

Ivor looked at him with a mirthless smile. He was by no means averse to the idea of fucking one or both of the pretty girls and normally he would have jumped at the chance. However, he was physically and mentally tired and would have far preferred to have postponed the joust until the next day. On the other hand, as Brian had rightly said, a promise was a promise, so despite feeling slightly weary, he started to undress. Perhaps Maggie's pussy would revitalise him as it had done so with the young footballer! When he was naked, Ruth threw up the eiderdown invitingly and Ivor climbed in beside her nude, warm body.

She turned her pretty face to his and, closing her liquid blue eyes, started to kiss him fiercely, sliding her tongue between his lips. Ivor pulled her even closer to him and returned the compliment, his hands kneading the fleshy cheeks of her backside as his tongue flashed inside her mouth.

Ruth took hold of his hand and pressed it against one of her lusciously rounded breasts and she whispered: 'Kiss my breasts, Ivor, I love having my titties sucked.'

He duly obliged and nibbled at the superbly fashioned

hard, tawny nipple whilst Ruth slipped her hand down to grasp his fully erect cock. They lay entwined together as he licked and sucked at her lovely titties, running his hands along her thighs. Ruth moved herself sideways so that he could insert one hand between her legs and stroke the damp curly hair of her bush before sliding a questing finger into her slit.

Now she moved across and over him so that her pussy was above his face as Ruth lowered her head and planted a full, wet kiss on the uncapped, rounded helmet of his pulsating shaft. Her soft hands caressed his hairy balls as, with a delicious slowness, she lapped up and around the length of his thick prick, letting her tongue dwell lovingly on his veiny shaft.

'Suck my knob, Ruth,' he panted and the willing girl obligingly kissed his domed bell-end, encircling it with the tip of her wet tongue before suddenly engulfing his knob inside her mouth, cramming in almost all of his cock between her lips and gobbling noisily on her fleshy lollipop.

Ruth now manoeuvred her knees on both sides of Ivor's body and lowered herself upon him. Her pussy pressed against Ivor's mouth. He licked furiously at the dripping crack, moving around the outer lips and gently slid a finger in and out of her cunny hole until the juices began to flow into his open mouth. He swallowed the tangy love liquid and then pulled his head away and panted: 'Let's change positions because otherwise I'll come in your mouth and I'd rather fuck your cunt with my cock.'

Obediently, she lifted herself off him and with a final swirling lick, opened her mouth and released his straining shaft. She presented her back to him and he squeezed the rounded cheeks of her lovely bottom. He turned his head to see Brian on top of Maggie, who had her legs wrapped round the photographer's waist as he jerked his hips forwards and backwards, his hands cupping her bum cheeks, pulling her towards him with each forward stroke.

Ivor thought for a moment and then he slid out of the bed with his cock standing high and huge against his flat belly. 'Ruth, let's fuck doggie-style and give Maggie and Brian a little more room,' he suggested to her. 'Jump out and stand in front of me, facing the bed. Now bend forwards, pushing out your bum.'

Again, Ruth was pleased to follow his orders and Ivor licked his lips as she leaned forward on her elbows, enjoying the sight of Brian and Maggie fucking each other as she thrust her bottom out towards him.

With trembling hands he parted the soft globes and Ruth gasped as she felt the hot shaft of his cock wedge itself in the crevice between her bum cheeks. Ivor pushed his knob through until he reached the glistening crack of her cunt. Then, as he thrust forward deeply, the girl whimpered with pleasure. He buried his thick shaft to the very hilt so that his heavy balls banged against her backside. First he wrapped his arms around her waist until his cock was fully embedded. Then he shifted his hands upwards to fondle her superb, uptilted breasts, rubbing the red rosebuds until they were as hard as his prick which was sliding so beautifully to and fro inside her clinging sheath.

Ruth turned her head and said in a fierce whisper: 'Go on, Ivor, fuck away, I want to feel every inch of your big fat cock ramming into me!' She wriggled her bottom and Ivor began to thrust backwards and forwards. He could feel Ruth explode into a running series of peaks of pleasure and her cunt felt incredibly tight and wet as her muscles contracted so deliciously around his cock.

They were lost in time as he filled her cunt with his

throbbing rock-hard rammer, sliding forward, withdrawing and then thrusting forward again until his shaft spewed out spasm after spasm of hot, sticky cream inside her willing love channel. To his surprise, his gleaming wet shaft was still erect! Ruth turned round, gasping with pleasure and grabbed his tool. Rubbing it between her palms, she said: 'Now it's my turn to call the shots – don't worry though, I know you must be exhausted so I'll do most of the work. Just lie back and let me play with your gorgeous cock. I'd like to give you a blow job that you'll never forget.'

'I won't argue with that,' said Ivor as he lay back on the pillow. Ruth tossed back her mane of strawberry blonde hair and knelt down between his legs. She laid her head on his thigh and started kissing and licking his rampant rod, sucking and squeezing his cock whilst his balls bounced up and down in front of her face. Her tongue circled his knob and her teeth scraped the tender flesh as she drew him between her rich, red lips, letting her tongue travel all the way up the length of his stiff shaft and teasing the underside of the plump, purple helmet.

Just then, Brian Lipman began to moan and Ivor turned his head to watch the photographer's body crash down on Maggie as he spurted his spunk. Maggie screamed out loud and clawed his wide back as she too reached the heights whilst Brian shuddered all over as he ejaculated his frothy seed inside her.

This erotic sight made Ivor's cock throb even more violently as he lay on his back, his thick prick pulsing with excitement whilst Ruth sucked lustily on his shaft. Using her face, tongue and lips only, she manoeuvred her mouth up and down over the smooth, distended mushroomed knob. Her mouth was hot, her tongue rough in a sandpapery way as it slicked across his helmet to the sensitive underside. A low growl escaped from his throat as Ruth opened her mouth and released his glistening cock. Athletically, she jumped across him and leaned forward, trailing her delectable soft breasts up and down his torso so that her rubbery nipples flicked exquisitely against his skin. Then she lifted her hips and crouched over his erection, her pouting love lips poised above his knob. She clasped his cock and pressed it directly over her clitty and by rotating her groin and edging slightly forward, she allowed his rigid rod to enter her.

Ruth purred with pleasure as, ever so slowly, she lifted and lowered her sopping slit, moving her bottom around the fulcrum of his stiff boner, her cunny muscles clinging firmly to his cock. He drove upwards to meet her downward plunges, driving his sturdy shaft even deeper inside her sheath. Ruth wiggled her bum cheeks wildly as they pushed and heaved, urging their bodies onwards. The perspiration began to form on Ivor's brow as he panted: 'I'm in you, Ruth, every inch of my big cock is crammed in your cunny! And now I'm going to spunk inside your tight little cunt!'

'Yes, yes, go on then, Ivor, shoot your load,' she cried out. Ivor felt her cunny muscles ripple along the length of his shaft and he gripped the cheeks of her bum, straining hard against her until the sweet sensation of his climax coursed through his body and his fierce spurts of spunk coated the walls of Ruth's tingling love channel.

When he had recovered, Ivor said gently: 'I'd love to stay here longer but believe it or not, I do have some things to do. Brian, I hope you haven't forgotten that we have a dinner date this evening with those two executives from Websters supermarkets?'

Brian looked at him blankly. 'A dinner date with two executives? What are you on about?' Then he snapped his fingers and groaned: 'Oh yes, I remember now. Is it really important though that I make an appearance, Ivor? I know that you're committed but I wouldn't have thought it was vital for me to show up.'

'Sorry, mate, but I'm afraid it is, especially as there's a possible new account also riding on this meeting. Look here, girls, I must drag Brian away but you're both invited to this thrash the journalists are throwing tonight, aren't you?'

'All being well, we'll see you there at around eleven,' said Ivor as he hurriedly flung on his clothes.

Maggie sat up and said: 'You mean the leaving party Ken and his friends are giving for Steve Elsey? Yes, I mentioned that we'd already been invited. Beth Rokeby told you about it whilst we were having a drink. But we've another party to go to, so make my excuses to Ken, please, if I don't show up.'

'Okay then, I'll say goodbye. But perhaps we'll meet up later. Brian, I'll take my leave and tidy up a few bits and pieces. Let's *rendezvous* in the bar at seven fifteen sharp, okay?'

'Aye, aye, captain,' said the photographer and he hugged the two girls close to him. 'You heard the man, my loves, duty calls. But I've still got thirty minutes left for a spot of rumpy-pumpy so shut the door behind you, Ivor, if you please, and I'll see you later on at the bar.'

Ivor acknowledged the request with a wave and made his way back to his room. He also had time for one more bout with Brian and the two pretty girls but he was pleasantly tired from his exertions with Ruth and it made more sense to have a short snooze and then luxuriate in a warm bath before changing for dinner, especially as Chrissie and Beth would both be expecting him to make love to them afterwards. He lay down on his bed and

94

picked up a copy of *The Scotsman* which was delivered every morning with the compliments of the hotel management. He smiled as he read that the Customs and Excise Commissioners had changed the tax rules on women's clothing because of the popularity of 'above the knee' dresses in the style made famous by the fashion model, Jean Shrimpton.

A great fan of the new mini-skirts, Ivor grinned as he read on: 'Up till now, length has been used to distinguish between women's dresses on which purchase tax of 10% of the wholesale value must be paid, and children's clothes which are tax free. But with hemlines still rising, a bust measurement has been added, so that in future a dress will not be exempt from purchase tax if it is more than thirty six inches round the chest or marked for any bust size more than thirty two inches.'

Ronnie Bloom will be marking all his thirty-three and thirty-four inch bust dresses as thirty-twos, reflected Ivor, making a mental note to call the rag trade tycoon who had been one of Cable Publicity's first clients when Martin Reece opened for business back in 1962. Ivor had enjoyed many a fling with the luscious models Brian Lipman used to hire when he took photographs of Ronnie's summer and winter collections. He drifted into a doze whilst he recalled the party at the Carlton Hotel in Cannes to celebrate Ronnie's new swimwear. It had culminated in a frenzied orgy in Martin's suite during which the highlight for Ivor was being fellated by a lithe black girl from Martinique whilst he lapped at the fluffy flaxen pussy of a curvy blonde who was busy jerking off Ronnie with one hand and a Saudi Arabian sheik with the other.

Ivor's cat nap was interrupted by the ring of the telephone by the side of his bed. 'Hello, Ivor Belling,' he said sleepily, wondering who might be calling him.

'Hello there, Ivor, it's Chrissie,' said a soft, sexy female voice. 'Good news, we promised our boss a hand job tomorrow if he'd let us leave early tonight, so we can be with you and Brian at about seven o'clock.'

'Lucky old boss – we'll look forward to seeing you, Chrissie, but I'm still working on a report. Can we meet at half past seven in the bar?'

'Okay, but I'm warning you that we're hungry, and I don't just mean for food. I'm ready and waiting for you, lover! My pussy wants to be filled with your big hard cock whilst you stroke my breasts and fuck me nice and slow like you did last night. It's so sexy the way you pull out your cock and then go in again even deeper.

'Oooh, I'm getting wet just talking about it. I wish you were here and you could slide your shaft inside my cunt and begin fucking me straight away. How does that sound to you, Ivor, would you like that, h'mm? Gosh, I'm so wound up that I'll have to bring myself off with my vibrator.'

Despite himself, his flaccid prick began to stir and Ivor drew a deep breath. 'Don't start without me,' he begged her as he looked at his fast-swelling penis. 'We'll not only fuck ourselves silly but we'll see if we can get Paula and Brian to join in for a whoresome foursome.'

'I don't think that'll prove very difficult. Paula loves cock as much as I do,' she breathed sensuously. 'Promise you'll be a good boy until I see you and don't ask any of the chambermaids to plate you before I arrive.'

He heard Chrissie blow a kiss down the line before she rang off. Gritting his teeth, Ivor resisted the temptation to frig his erect prick. He swung himself off the bed and walked to the bathroom to begin his pre-prandial preparations.

❁ THREE ❁

Glasgow Belongs To Me

Shortly after seven o'clock, Ivor sat himself down on a stool at the plush restaurant bar and ordered himself a large gin and tonic. Fifteen minutes later he was joined by Brian Lipman who still looked slightly bleary-eyed even after a refreshing cold shower and a change of clothes.

'Honestly Brian, you shouldn't have fucked Maggie again after I left. No wonder you look like you've been under the cosh!' said Ivor severely. 'Remember, I mustn't fall out with Chrissie tonight as I want her to introduce me to her brother-in-law. Incidentally, I spoke about Jetstream to Martin. Craig Grey will be in Edinburgh in a couple of days for some conference or other. He'll stay on and help me blind these shower manufacturers with all the facts and figures to show that we know what we're talking about.'

'Lots of luck, pal! I wish I could stay for another couple of days but I'm catching the eight o'clock flight back to London tomorrow and get all the stuff I've shot up here processed. Don't worry about tonight, though. I'll be okay, there's nothing that a decent meal won't put right. It's all very well for you to talk, but I only had a couple of measly sandwiches at lunchtime before I had to go off to the supermarket with the girls. Anyhow, your problem isn't going to be with whether I keep Paula satisfied in bed but how you're going to keep both Chrissie and Beth happy at the party – and who you're going to bring back here afterwards.'

Ivor pulled at his cheek and slowly nodded his head. 'You're quite right, it is going to be a problem,' he admitted as Brian called the waiter over and ordered an orange juice. 'I'm hoping that, with a bit of luck, one of them will get pulled by one of the press boys – and then I'll be able to slip away with the other.

'We'll just have to play it by ear,' he added as he rose to his feet. Chrissie and Paula were making their way towards the bar. Brian also scrambled up to greet the girls.

'Hi there, you both look stunning,' said Ivor with genuine appreciation. He noticed several male heads turn to stare at the two attractive girls. Chrissie's mane of light blonde hair tumbled down the sides of her face and onto the shoulders of a black dress styled with a six-inch-above-the-knee hemline which, as Ivor had read an hour before in the newspaper, had caused the Customs and Excise people to change their Purchase Tax regulations. And the dark haired Paula looked equally ravishing in a tight green off-the-shoulder dress which accentuated her lush breasts and slim waist as she walked across to the bar.

'What would you like to drink?' enquired Ivor. After ordering a vodka and tonic for Chrissie and a Barcadi and cola for Paula, he slid off the bar stool and they sat at a table whilst, at Ivor's request, Brian went inside the restaurant to check their reservation.

When he returned and confirmed that all was in order,

Ivor cleared his throat and said: 'Girls, something's cropped up tonight –'

'What, already?' interrupted Chrissie and she and Paula exploded into a fit of giggles. 'You're a quick worker, that's for sure!'

'No, I'm keeping my powder dry at the moment,' Ivor continued patiently. He went on to explain how important it was for Brian and himself to go along to the press party after dinner. 'You're both invited as well,' he added hastily when he saw their faces fall. 'Although, of course, if you don't want to go with us, we'll quite understand.'

Paula's face brightened instantly. 'Of course we'll go with you to the party, it should be great fun,' she declared roundly. 'Chrissie and I love parties, don't we?'

'I should say,' said Chrissie with relief, 'that's good news, Ivor. Where did you say it's being held? Near the dental hospital? No problem, it's only five minutes away by taxi and we can get back here easy enough.'

Ivor gave her a glassy smile as the head waiter came up and handed out their menus. 'You choose, Ivor, I wouldn't know what half these things are even if this was written in English,' said Chrissie. She looked blankly down at the ornately written *table d'hôte*.

'Well, you can have what you like, but the set meal is Trout and Tuna Mousse, Roast Chicken in Lemon Sauce with New Potatoes, Grilled Tomatoes and French Beans, followed by a choice of sweets from the dessert trolley.'

'That sounds delicious,' she said promptly and Ivor ordered the same for himself. Paula and Brian both chose vegetable soup followed by a rump steak with chips as their main course. Feeling reckless, Ivor ordered a bottle of '62 vintage champagne although Brian Lipman blanched when he heard Ivor give the order. 'Here, that's very nice of you, mate, but the champagne's six quid a bottle! Won't Martin grumble about expenses now you can only claim tax relief when entertaining foreign buyers?'

'I'll put Chrissie and Paula down as foreign buyers,' answered Ivor. 'Well, they're Scottish aren't they? No seriously, Martin has a very useful couple of friends who work in Paris and we're allowed to use their names on bills on special occasions like tonight.'

'I had a wonderful French lover for a few weeks last year,' said Paula brightly. 'Jacques la Troquer, who was a visiting lecturer on international relations at Glasgow University. He loved to buy champagne, though he said it's much more expensive here than in France. Come to think of it, it was champagne that brought us together and though we didn't often drink it with meals, we often used to go to bed with a bottle.'

A broad smile broke out on her face as she recalled the passionate affair. Brian grunted: 'Come on, spill the beans, Paula. There's no call for me to be jealous, especially as I presume Monsieur Jacques is now back in France.'

'Yes, he only stayed in Glasgow for two months but we had a wild time together. Do you really want to hear about him? You do? Well, it all began when I met Jacques on a rainy Saturday afternoon at the Gibson Gallery. I've always been keen on looking at pictures and they were showing some marvellous works of Joseph Crawhall, a late nineteenth-century Scottish painter.'

'One of the Glasgow Boys group,' Brian interjected and Paula was duly impressed. 'You're interested in paintings then, Brian?' she asked and he replied proudly: 'I came top of my class in the history of art when I studied for my diploma at the Hornsey College of Design.'

'My, so you're not just a pretty face,' said Chrissie. Ivor added: 'He's not *even* a pretty face. Go on, Paula, carry on with the story.'

'Okay, though I'm glad that Crawhall has his admirers down south,' she continued. 'Well, I'd been in the Gallery for about half an hour and I was just about to leave when this big, handsome guy walked in. He was wearing a black leather jacket, boots, and tight black trousers. I noticed two other girls nudge each other and whisper between themselves when they caught sight of him.

'He stood in front of Crawhall's *The Flower Shop* and I went up bold as brass and asked him what he thought of it. He said that the work showed Crawhall's droll sense of humour and acute observation of nature. We chatted on whilst Mr Gibson generously served glasses of mulled wine to the thirty or so people in the gallery. Jacques turned out to be kind, courteous and intelligent. But then, as he passed by me with a tray of empty wine glasses, Mr Gibson accidently jogged my elbow which made me spill my drink on my blouse.

'"Oh no, a brand-new blouse and it's red wine too," I groaned but Jacques said: "A friend of mine works at the Theatre Royal and he gave me a tube of special stain remover which the wardrobe people use. If you would permit me, we can go back to my flat and we'll see what can be done."

'Naturally I was delighted to accept. I put on my coat and we left the gallery and although the sky was still a leaden grey, at least the rain had stopped. "Have you ever had a ride on a motor-bike?" Jacques asked and I told him that I had only ridden pillion on my brother's little Vespa which was nothing like Jacques' big, Japanese machine. I clung on to him as he drove back to his flat. I don't know why but something about all that power and hot steel between my legs made it a thrilling ride. By the time we arrived at his flat, the vibrations of the bike against my crotch had started to make me feel definitely receptive to the idea of sampling Jacques's French tickler!

'Once safely inside I took off my coat and jacket. He handed me a tube of this special stain remover and I rubbed some of the mixture over the stain. "May I have a hanger, Jacques, as it would be better for me to take the blouse off and let it dry," I asked.

'"*Certainement*," he replied and fetched one from his bedroom. I peeled off my blouse and I could see Jacques's face pale as he gazed upon my milky white breasts which were pressed into uplifted scalloped cup shells which barely covered my nipples. Jacques said nothing but looked into my eyes intently as I reached behind my back and unhooked my bra. Then he stepped forward and said softly in his sexy continental accent: "Paula, you are a most beautiful girl. What gorgeous breasts you have, so firm and yet so gently rounded." Then taking my head in his hands, he kissed me. And what a kiss! He probed my mouth with the tip of his tongue, sliding it slowly between my teeth and passing it in a caress around my gums. It aroused me even more especially when he slid the straps of my bra down my arms and rubbed my big stalky nipples between his fingers.

'I could feel my panties getting wet as I began to loosen his belt and he, in turn, expertly undressed me. When we were both naked, he lifted me up and carried me into his bedroom. He lay me down gently on the bed and then whispered: "*Un moment, cherie.*"'

The wine waiter appeared at this point and with a 'pop' opened the Moet et Chandon champagne which Ivor had ordered. He filled the glasses of the four diners. 'Cheers, everyone,' said Ivor and they clinked glasses before downing the chilled sparkling wine.

'That couldn't come at a more appropriate moment,' observed Paula as she set her glass down on the table. 'You see, Jacques reappeared half a minute later sporting a huge hard-on and carrying a bottle of exactly the same champagne as we're drinking now.

'"Lie back, *ma belle*," he said and he jumped on the bed between my legs and smoothed his hands over my thighs. Then he opened the bottle of champagne and poured the bubbly all over my body, letting it flow between my breasts and down over my tummy till it trickled down into my pussy bush. I looked at him in astonished surprise but he smiled wolfishly at me and murmured: "Even the finest vintage will taste better this way!" He leaned forward and started to lap up the bubbles first from my erect titties and then between my legs, licking up the mixture of my love juices and the vintage champagne!

'Oh, I so wish that British men would learn more about the sophisticated art of eating pussy from the French and Italians! I was soon in raptures as he quickly found my excitable little clitty which sent waves of passion spilling all through my body. My cunt was now sopping wet as I clasped my legs around his head. I felt an orgasm coming and I exploded with a scream. Then he made me burst out laughing as he began to hum the Marseillaise against my clitty. Funnily enough, the low notes made me come again whilst the high notes sent ripples running up and down my spine. It was fantastic but I simply couldn't go on any longer without being fucked.

'I trailed a finger up and down my crack and then slowly pulled the lips apart, holding my cunt open so that Jacques could see deep into my gash. He understood my needs and he lifted his handsome face from my dripping crack and hauled himself over me. I looked down at his cock which was thick, long and slightly curved. I grabbed hold of this rigid, veiny pole and guided the pulsating pole to my waiting cunt. He buried himself inside me with a deep strong thrust which mashed my clitty against his pubic bone. We lay together very still for a moment and then he started to stroke his shaft in and out of my soaking slit, penetrating me at a lightning force, ramming home with a will. I was almost delirious with pleasure as little climaxes raced round my body.

'We fucked away furiously. I stretched my legs round his hips as he thrust back and forth and I muttered fiercely that I wanted him to spunk inside me. We climaxed together as with a final shudder he shot a huge wad of sticky cream inside my juicy pussy.'

She finished her story with a sigh and, as if on cue, two waiters bustled round the table and served the starters. The two men had been visibly moved by Paula's tale and Brian slid his hand on Paula's knee and said to her: 'God Almighty! I can't wait to finish dinner and get you back to my room, you randy girl.'

Paula's story had also given Ivor a hard-on but he was still mulling over the problem of how he could solve the dilemma of his double date with Chrissie and Beth. If only I had an extra cock available, he said to himself, and to his delighted surprise, his reverie was broken by the fruity, familiar voice calling out: 'Ivor, Brian, how good to see you again!'

He looked up and saw the bulky figure of the Honourable Anthony Godfrey walking towards them. Ivor's face creased into a grin, for with luck, Tony Godfrey might prove to be the answer to all his troubles. Until his journey up on the night sleeper from London,

Ivor and Brian had only known of Tony Godfrey from the popular newspapers. The laid-back son of the multi-millionaire industrialist Lord Dartmouth was a gossip columnist's dream. Not a week passed by without his name being constantly linked with pretty girls, ranging from minor European royal princesses to the daughters of Home Counties colonels (more than one of whom had threatened to horse-whip him if he ever set foot in their homes again) and mini-skirted models whom he attracted like flies to an open jam-jar.

Ivor and Brian had met Tony on the train when they had become intimately acquainted with two girls and subsequently with Tony Godfrey and a luscious teenage folk singer in whom he had taken an interest.

'Tony, hi there, how's it all going?' said Ivor, shaking hands vigorously. 'Are you on your own or is that sexy young folk singer with you? Christ, I must be losing my marbles, but do you know, I've clean forgotten her name.'

'Wendy, you mean?' said Tony gloomily. 'East Dulwich's answer to Bob Dylan? No, I'm afraid we had a terrible argument. I told her that it would be best if we split up and she found herself a new manager.'

'What a pity, Wendy was a gorgeous looking girl,' Ivor commented. He rapidly explained to Chrissie and Paula how Tony had been helping Wendy further her singing career by bringing her up to Glasgow to audition for an important folk festival.

'Was she just a taker, then?' enquired Brian. According to the gossip columnists, it was well known that although generous by nature, Tony Godfrey was nobody's fool. He knew well enough that his exquisitely furnished mews house in Mayfair, smart apartment in New York and luxurious villa in St Tropez were among the reasons why so many attractive young women flocked round him. This did not bother him unduly, except when he felt that a girl was taking advantage of his generosity. But in this case it seemed that there was another reason for the falling out with his latest girl friend.

'No, it wasn't that at all, it was because –' and Tony blushed as his voice trailed away.

'Oh, you don't have to be bashful in front of Chrissie and Paula,' said Ivor, and he introduced the heir to the Dartmouth millions to the two girls. 'Come and sit down and tell us about it.'

Chrissie looked hard at Tony as she shook hands with him and said: 'This is exciting, meeting a real life celebrity. I've read an awful lot about you in the papers, Tony. It was only about a week ago that they said you're supposed to be getting engaged to that pretty little Spanish singer who won the European Song Contest last year.'

'Never believe what you read in the papers, my dear. These days I only have to be seen with a girl and the gossip columnists are already marrying me off,' he replied with a smile.

'So why did you break up with, what's her name, Wendy, this girl who Ivor was talking about?' asked Paula as Chrissie filled a tumbler with champagne for the new arrival.

Tony raised his glass. 'Good health, everybody,' he said as he took a sip. 'M'mm, what's the celebration folks? This stuff's the real McCoy.'

'Why don't you join us for dinner, Tony? Draw up another chair, there's plenty of room at the table,' Ivor interrupted as he called over the head waiter. 'And I'll order another bottle of bubbly.'

'Are you sure? As it happens I was just going to grab a quick bite before meeting an old chum who lives up here. But he's just cried off as he's had to work late so I'm free this evening. So thank you, Ivor, I accept with pleasure.'

Ivor instructed the head waiter to lay another place for Tony and he said: 'Good, that's settled then. Now you can tell us all about Wendy.'

'Well, it's a strange business, that's for sure. I suppose the simple fact of the matter is that she's a high-spirited exhibitionist and I found it impossible to control her.'

'I would have thought that all performers were of that tendency,' remarked Brian. 'After all, if you weren't keen on showing off, you'd hardly be likely to make a career in showbiz.'

'Fair enough,' Tony agreed and he paused for a moment to tell the head waiter that he would have the *table d'hote* meal. Then he continued: 'But Wendy has, what shall I call it, this carnal craving and she hasn't yet learned that there's a right time and a right place to satisfy it.'

His audience looked puzzled and he went on: 'I'll give you an example. The other day after lunch, we went upstairs to her room (we're staying at the Grand, incidentally) and had a good fuck. Then a few minutes later she made me lie on my back, knelt between my legs and gave me a long French kiss. Then she worked her tongue down my body, stopping at my groin, of course, and sucked my cock for what seemed like ages – not that I was complaining!

'When I came, she swallowed all my spunk and she wanted me to fuck her again. Frankly, I would have needed a bit of time to recover and besides that, we had an appointment to keep with a concert promoter on the other side of the city. Traffic was very bad because some visiting dignitary was in town and he was being driven in procession to see the Lord Mayor, so the hotel porter advised us to take the underground train.

'Well, we weren't the only people with the same idea and the carriage was filling up by the time we boarded the train. However, Wendy and I both managed to find seats. By the next stop, new passengers had to stand and they were squashed together like in the middle of the rush hour. I was feeling a bit tired after our fuck so I half-closed my eyes and dozed as the train ground to a halt in the tunnel between stations. I looked around but nobody was alarmed and they all appeared to be lost in their own little worlds – reading, dozing or staring into space.

'I turned to speak to Wendy and I nearly jumped out of my skin! She'd unbuttoned her coat and she'd pulled her denim hot pants high over her crossed legs. She hadn't put on a bra and I could see her erect nipples through her T-shirt. I could see that she was staring hard at the bulging crotch of a strapping young fellow of about twenty who was standing smack in front of her. Then I saw her hand snake forward . . .'

Beads of perspiration appeared on Tony's forehead and he mopped his brow before he continued: 'Sure enough, she unzipped his fly and she squirmed her bottom against the seat as she brought out his cock and sucked him off right there and then. Thank God nobody seemed to have noticed what was going on as she teased his pink knob with her tongue until with a short gasp, he spunked inside her mouth and she gulped down his jism. Well, she popped the youngster's limp, wet shaft back inside his jeans and he zipped himself up. There was a blissful smile on his face, but I was appalled! I said nothing until we arrived at our station but when we were walking across the road to the promoter's office, I angrily told Wendy how I felt about her behaviour. "All you need is one court conviction for indecency and your career will be over before it's begun," I said to her. "Whatever possessed you to suck off a perfect stranger?"

'She tossed her head and replied: "Well, if you must know, he wasn't a perfect stranger. Didn't you recognise Tommy? He's one of the assistant porters at the hotel. I'd fancied him ever since I clapped eyes on him. And as for doing it in public, okay, it was a bit dangerous but I don't make a habit of it, though I do love an element of surprise in fucking. I don't like *anything* in my life to be routine and I like funny, outrageous men who don't know what the word inhibition means!"

'Anyhow, one word led to another and although we completed our business with the impresario, we decided that evening to split up. Very sad perhaps, and strange really, because I've been called many things in my time but never a puritan or a kill-joy. Let's face it, I love fucking as much if not more than the next man, and I've had some pretty wild experiences myself. But you can't mix business and pleasure and I have to say that as far as I'm concerned there's no point in any further involvement with Wendy.'

The waiters brought Tony's *hors d'oeuvres* and he smacked his lips and said: 'This fish mousse is delicious.' As he tucked in, Ivor was happy to see that Chrissie was obviously taken with Tony Godfrey.

He allowed himself a tiny grunt of agreement when he heard her say to Tony: 'I also love sex but I do agree with you that there's a right time and place for everything, even a good fuck.'

'Or especially a good fuck,' said Brian genially as a

phalanx of waiters descended on the party and served up their main course. The food was delicious and by the time their plates were cleared away, Ivor and his guests had finished not only the second but also the third bottle of champagne.

Chrissie pushed back her chair and announced: 'Will you excuse me, but I must go to the little girls' room.'

This was the opportunity Ivor had been waiting for and he said: 'I'll go with you, Chrissie, I need to point Percy at the porcelain myself.'

When he reached the cloakrooms, he edged her to one side and said softly: 'Look, love, I want to put my cards on the table. I can see that you fancy Tony Godfrey and I want you to know that I don't mind at all if you get off with him tonight. It's not that I don't want to have you to myself –'

She finished the sentence for him. 'But you want to have a free hand at the party tonight,' she said, nudging him in the ribs. 'It's all right, I quite understand. There might be one or two women writers who you need to butter up. Actually, this gives me the chance to say that I'd rather not go to the party at all. You see, I knew about this booze-up before you mentioned it. One of the guys organising the party was at the supermarket this afternoon and he invited me along. Frankly he might be more than a wee bit miffed if he doesn't get a chance to take me home – which wouldn't do you any good, would it?

'I like him, Ivor, and once you've gone I'll go out with this guy. I want to have an honest open relationship with him but we'll never get it off the ground if he remembers seeing you and I leaving the party together. So you see, I would honestly prefer it if Tony and I could slope off after dinner, especially now I know that this wouldn't upset your evening.'

110

Ivor breathed a sigh of relief. 'Have no worries on the score – frankly, it would probably be the best thing all round if you and Tony made your excuses when it's time for us to go,' he said candidly. 'Brian and Ruth can do as they like, it won't affect me what they decide to do, but I must be free to push the bloody product to the pressmen and also I don't want to upset Ken or his sister, come to think of it. We would like her support in the continuing public relations campaign for Four Seasons.'

'Say no more, Ivor, we've had a grand time and I just hope that we'll see each other again on your next trip to Scotland,' she said generously as she swept into the ladies' powder room.

By the time they returned to the table Brian Lipman was about to regale Paula and Tony Godfrey about some unexpected fun that came his way on a cross channel ferry the previous summer. 'Sorry, Ivor, you've heard this before, but Tony and the girls don't know the story,' he said with a chuckle. 'You reminded me of it, Ruth, when you said how you never missed an episode of that new TV series about a private eye, *Mountjoy and Company*, with Martin Elstree and Valerie Allendale.

'How it all happened was like this – last year National Television were trying to sell the series to the Yanks, so they wanted someone to take some publicity stills whilst they were shooting Martin uncovering a smuggling racket on board a cruise liner between Rio and France. Well, the night before they're due to travel, the TV crew's photographer went down with 'flu and so the producer called me up and asked if I could fill in at short notice. I didn't have too much on and I rather fancied the job so I packed a bag and was down in Dover by mid-morning, where the ship would call before heading for Marseilles that afternoon.

'Naturally, everything had been arranged with the ship's captain and crew. The director was happy to use the ordinary passengers in crowd scenes, they weren't allowed to get too close because their chatter and clicking of their cameras would upset the sound track. Naturally, that didn't apply to me and I had access to the sets at all times. It was great fun, especially when the sun came out just when they were going to shoot a scene by the swimming pool. Mike Lewis, the director, told four of the female extras we had on board to get changed quickly into their swimming costumes and asked me to take some publicity shots of the girls draping themselves around Martin Elstree. I'd been too busy to notice these girls before, but they came back in the tiniest bikinis you could ever imagine! Well, if I say so myself, it takes an extraordinary woman to make my eyes water – not that I'm *blasé* you understand – but at least three days a week I'm photographing pretty girls wearing little or nothing . . .'

'No wonder you catch colds in the winter!' joked Ivor.

Brian chuckled: 'No, it's not very often that I undress though I won't deny that occasionally I've stripped off before a session so that the model wouldn't feel uncomfortable about being nude whilst I kept my clothes on!

'Anyhow, these three birds were all gorgeous but the most stunning was a young girl called Stephanie who was wearing a white bikini. She was quite tall, five foot nine or even ten, with long dark hair which fell down to the middle of her back. Her breasts weren't huge but I could see the outline of her large pert nipples which strained against the material of her bikini top. Her body was well-proportioned and she had the cutest little bum you could ever wish to pinch.

112

'And I soon found out that I wasn't the only one who found Stephanie so attractive! Mike Lewis muttered something to me about making sure I shot some good photos of her and Martin Elstree was laying on the charm, saying how good she looked and asking her if she had ever worked in television before. I can tell you that Rosie Blaney-Ford, the girl who plays Martin's secretary in the series and who he'd been shagging for the last three months, was very put out. She dragged Martin off the set when I'd finished! Mike Lewis noticed that Rosie was smouldering so he muttered to me: "Brian, do me a favour and get the girl away from Martin or I'm going to be in trouble," because he didn't want any flare-ups between members of the cast.

'"Leave it to me, Mike," I said and I went across to Stephanie, tapped her on the shoulder and introduced myself. I said to Martin: "Sorry to take Stephanie away but I need her for some solo publicity photographs." I steered Stephanie away to the bar, and I ordered us drinks. Like all actresses, she knew the value of publicity and when I told her that I would probably be able to place her picture in the *Daily Sketch*, her eyes lit up and she thanked me a million times. "I love having my photograph taken," she said eagerly. "My boy friend Jeff took some colour transparencies which he wants to send to *Playboy* but I don't think they're good enough."

'"If you'd like me to give you a professional opinion about them, pop them in the post or better still come down to my studio in London," I suggested. "Oh, would you, Brian?" she said. "But I've got them here on board in my case. Would you possibly have time to look at them now?"

'She didn't have to ask twice! When we finished our drinks, I followed her downstairs to her cabin. We sat on the bed whilst I looked at the trannies which, as Stephanie had realised, weren't of professional quality. But my cock almost burst out of my trousers when I held one particular trannie up to the light. It showed Stephanie lying naked on a hammock strung between two trees. She was half-turned towards the camera and I drooled over her lovely breasts but she had her left hand spread over her groin so I could only glimpse a few wisps of pussy hair between her long fingers.

'"You're quite right, these trannies aren't good enough to send to a top-class magazine, but you look terrific in front of a camera," I said to her. "I'll offer you a decent contract here and now to pose for a nudie spread. I'd send the photos to *Playboy* and I also scout for other men's magazines in America, Europe and the Far East. No guarantees, Steph, but I think you must be looking at a thousand pounds at least for an afternoon's work."

'Stephanie was thrilled and we went upstairs and celebrated with another drink. "Here's to fame and fortune," I said, as we clinked glasses. I was staring so hard at this sexy dolly bird that I spilt half of my drink into my lap! Stephanie wiped off the Scotch with her hand and as she squeezed my throbbing erection she leaned forward and whispered in my ear: "I think we should get out of here before you knock over a table with that iron bar between your legs, don't you?"

'Once back inside her cabin, she plastered herself up against me and whilst we kissed she ran her tongue all around my mouth before plunging it inside. I unbuckled my belt but she pulled my hands away. "I want to undress you," she said softly as she unhooked her top and let her uptilted round breasts bounce free. Those strawberry nipples were already sticking out, just begging to be sucked! I bent my head forward but again she stopped me and then she unbuttoned my shirt and folded it neatly over a chair. She kissed and nibbled my nipples and trailed kisses downwards as she pulled off my trousers.

'As soon as I was naked, she crouched down and rubbed my pulsing prick against her tits. "I'm going to come if you do that," I said hoarsely but this only made Stephanie smile and take my prick between her lips. She swirled her tongue round the knob and one wash across was all it needed and with a woosh, I came inside her mouth. She gulped down my jism and I staggered over to the bed where I watched her tug down her bikini bottoms and the sight of her peachy bum made my shaft tingle and swell up again.

'Stephanie wiggled her bum and then turned round and without further ado she came over to the bed and climbed on top of me with her knees on either side. She pulled open her pussy lips with her fingers and began rubbing herself on the tip of my cock. I was bucking and heaving like crazy, trying to slide my prick up into her cunt. She teased me for a moment or two but then she lifted herself up. With a saucy glint in her eye, she crashed down on my quivering cock, tightening her cunny muscles to keep me in place as she rocked backwards and forwards, slicking my shaft with her juices as she moaned with ecstasy.

'I reached up and tweaked her big red nipples and cupped her bum cheeks as she bounced up and down on my tadger. "Go on, big boy, cream my cunt," she gasped as she contracted her cunny walls with my cock inside her. This sent a long rippling seizure running from the root to the very tip of my prick. "Yes! Yes! Yes!" I cried out and I thrust up so hard that she had a job to keep my cock inside her as our bodies twisted and writhed on the narrow bed. Stephanie ground her pussy against me and her teeth sank into my shoulder. With an enormous shudder, she climaxed and I pushed upwards once more and pumped a flood of hot spunk inside her sopping slit.

'I lay back and she leaned forwards with my now shrivelled shaft still inside her juicy crack and she kissed me on the mouth. "Well done, Brian! That was a super fuck!" she murmured whilst I lay panting with exhaustion.'

There was a momentary silence as the photographer refreshed himself with a huge swig of champagne. Chrissie wriggled uncomfortably in her seat and said: 'You are naughty, Brian, you've made me feel so randy that I don't think I'll bother going to the party after we've finished eating.

'I'll just have to go back home and play with myself,' she sighed as she slid a hand under the table and ran her fingers along Tony Godfrey's thigh. 'Ivor must make an appearance at the party as he has work to do and you and Paula should go too, you'll enjoy it.'

Tony Godfrey cleared his throat. 'If I may be so bold,' he said nervously, 'I'd far prefer to have a quiet night-cap with you rather than go to this party which Ivor, Brian and Paula are off to. The only problem is that my hotel is very peculiar about guests entertaining visitors in their rooms.'

'What a pity,' Chrissie frowned as she continued to stroke Tony's thigh, 'because my flat-mate is making dinner for her boy friend and I don't really want to play gooseberry by coming home too early.'

'Well, you can watch TV and have a drink in my room,' said Ivor, fishing out his key. 'There's a mini-bar by the wardrobe so you can tuck yourselves away and not be disturbed. I won't be back till God knows when, if at all, so you can stay all night as far as I'm concerned.'

'That's very decent of you, Ivor,' said Tony Godfrey warmly, unaware of course that the others were playing out a little charade for their mutual benefit. 'How does that sound to you, Chrissie?'

'Great, it would solve all our problems,' she enthused, grasping Tony's semi-erect shaft and giving it a friendly squeeze. 'Thanks, Ivor, once we're inside one of us will pop down and leave the key at reception so you can collect it whenever you return.'

Soon afterwards the happy group broke up. Tony and Chrissie waved the others goodbye as they clambered into a cab for the short journey to Renfrew Street. 'Hell, I forgot to bring a bottle,' said Ivor but Brian pulled out a bottle of whisky from the voluminous pocket of his raincoat and grunted: 'Just as well that I remembered, then. This bottle of Johnny Walker should get us in without any bother.'

It was now almost a quarter past eleven but, as Beth Rokeby had forecast, the party was only beginning to gather a head of steam when they arrived. The bottle of Johnny Walker was warmly received by the host and immediately opened to drink a toast to Steve Elsey, the young photographer who was leaving for the Manchester office of the *Daily Mirror*.

Beth slipped her arm round Ivor and pulled him to one side. She kissed his ear and said softly: 'I'm so pleased you managed to ditch your supermarket guests. What excuse did you make?'

'Luckily, we didn't have to,' replied Ivor shamelessly. 'They wanted to get home after dinner and I certainly wasn't going to dissuade them.'

'And I bet young Paula is delighted that Brian Lipman was free to bring her to the party,' she went on. 'But where's Chrissie? My brother Ken will be awfully disappointed if she doesn't show up.'

'Oh, just as well you reminded me about her, I'm afraid

she phoned earlier on to say she had a bit of a headache,' he fibbed adroitly, 'and she asked me to tell Ken that she'd call him tomorrow. Shall we do that now before we forget?'

'Okay,' said Beth but they were waylaid by Brian who said: 'Sorry, Beth, but can I borrow Ivor for a minute or two? I want him to meet John Gibson of the *Edinburgh Evening News* who'll be leaving for home soon.'

'Of course you can, Brian. I'll have a word with Ken whilst you two sing the praises of Four Seasons to John.'

Ivor and Brian worked their way round the guests, giving out information packs and free tins of Four Seasons to anyone who wanted them. When Ivor rejoined Beth she was deep in conversation with an older man whom she introduced as Freddie from the *Evening Express*.

It was immediately apparent to Ivor that, from his dishevelled appearance and the slight slurring of his words, Freddie had drunk a little more than was good for him. But Beth winked and said: 'Freddie's been telling me a very interesting story. Go on, Freddie, Ivor would also like to hear about how you keep your wife satisfied.'

'He would, would he?' said Freddie as he slumped down into an armchair. Ivor and Beth perched on the arms and bent forward to listen to the slightly sozzled journalist. 'Well, your brother Ken knows the score, Beth,' he said. 'I married my wife three years ago when I was thirty five and Donna was twenty two. She was a convent girl and had never had sex till we met up, but ever since we got married, she's been insatiable.

'Don't misunderstand me, I love the way she takes every opportunity to fuck. The other week we had sex in a bus shelter after coming out of the cinema and when we went out for a fish supper two nights ago, she sucked me off whilst I was eating my chips in a shop doorway on the

Great Western Road. To be honest with you, I'm finding it impossible to keep up with her.

'Last night after dinner she sucked me off before we had a good fuck. Then we decided to have a drink down at our pub. Donna had taken off her panties and after only half an hour in the bar she told me that her pussy was tingling and needed a good seeing-to.

'"Give us a break, who do you think I am, Supercock? If you're that desperate for a shag, what about giving a good time to those lads playing bar billiards," I said jokingly. But Donna took me at my word and looked up at the two youngsters. She licked her lips and said: "I'd love to, Freddie, and I'm sure you'd enjoy watching me screw them."

'I thought she was just trying to excite me but there was a gleam in her eyes and I'd never seen her look so excited. "Okay, let's see what we can do," I said and we got talking to the two boys, one of whom was fair-haired and the other so dark-skinned I wondered if he might be a half-caste. Anyway, I saw her feeling them up though I pretended not to have seen anything, and they were more than happy to come back to our house for a few more drinks. I made an excuse to leave them in the lounge, saying I had some work I had to finish upstairs in my study.

'About twenty minutes later, I tip-toed down the stairs. I thought they might be up to something but I didn't want to spoil it by walking straight in on them so I quietly opened the door a fraction and peeked round to see what was happening. My timing couldn't have been better!

'Donna was stark naked and was busy getting fucked. The youths were naked as well and the sandy haired lad was lying down on the floor and Donna was on top of him with his cock right up her cunt whilst she was gobbling the

119

dark boy's thick prick. Within minutes, both of them were shooting their loads up her and into her mouth whilst I looked on with a huge hard-on pressing against my trousers.

'When they had finished, my wife called out: "Come on, Freddie, it's your turn now," and so I stripped off whilst my wife scrambled up and sat in a chair with her pussy wide open and the love juice dribbling down her thighs. Donna still wanted more cock so I obliged and we both enjoyed a tremendous fuck whilst she wanked off the two young fellas, taking a cock in each hand whilst I pumped away into her pussy. The boys got dressed and left and we went to bed and somehow I found the strength to fuck her once more before we went to sleep.'

'What a night! If Donna needs as much sex as this, Freddie, it's no wonder that you look so tired,' said Beth sympathetically.

'Aye, you're right there, lassie,' he agreed as he mopped his brow. 'She's a wonderful girl but I can't satisfy her by myself. Ken Barret helped me out a couple of times and we met the dark lad I was telling you about again in the pub and occasionally he comes back to our house for a threesome, but the problem is finding somebody to fuck Donna on a regular basis. And that's not so easy as it sounds, though if necessary I'd be prepared to pay the chap's travelling expenses.'

Ivor spread out his hands and remarked: 'It certainly isn't so easy as it sounds – I mean, at first you'd think it simple to find a chap who'd be willing to fuck a sexy girl like Donna twice a week. But let's face it, you wouldn't want to engage any Tom, Dick or Harry to fuck your wife.'

'Especially any Dick,' said a pleasant female voice from behind him. Ivor swung round to see an attractive curvy girl in her mid twenties standing behind him. 'Hi there, I'm Donna, Freddie's wife. Has he been telling you that story about how I'm so insatiable that he has to bring home young men to fuck me?'

Ivor blushed and looked back at Freddie who was now fast asleep in his chair. 'Well, Freddie was rambling on a bit about your unusual sex life,' he admitted apologetically but Donna waved away his embarrassment. 'Don't worry, I'm used to it. He always does this when he's had too much to drink, poor love. You mustn't believe a word of it, of course. The trouble is that Freddie has got it into his head that he can't satisfy me – he believes that his prick is too small, that he comes too quickly and so I always have to fake an orgasm.'

'Good grief, how awful for you,' said Beth as she slowly exhaled a deep breath. 'Poor Freddie covers up his own inadequacies by pretending that your insatiability causes all the difficulties.'

Donna smiled ruefully and said with a shrug: 'Well, it isn't very nice to know that when he's had a few drinks, your husband is telling anyone who'll listen to him that you're suffering from satyriasis. And what makes it worse is that all Freddie's problems are in his mind, not in his groin. There's nothing wrong with his equipment – I'm no expert on pricks but I do know that Freddie's shaft fits beautifully into my pussy. Although I don't come every time we make love, I always enjoy it and there's absolutely no reason for him to feel inadequate.

'Honestly, why you men are obsessed by the size of your cocks has always been beyond me,' she said to Ivor. She lifted her glass and swallowed down a large draught of Brian Lipman's Scotch.

'Oh, be fair now,' said Ivor indignantly. 'You girls are no different when it comes to the size of your boobs.'

'*Touché, monsieur*, and I suppose in Freddie's case a lot of the damage was done by his parents. His father was a very strict, authoritarian kind of man and his mother was very religious. Between the two of them, they fucked up poor Freddie's sexual life. They told him his cock would fall off if he didn't stop wanking and I'm sure that even now when we're having a good fuck, a wee little anxious voice deep down in his subconscious is telling him that it's sinful to enjoy himself in bed.'

'Well, what's the solution? You can't go on like this,' said Beth. Donna nodded and replied: 'I've finally persuaded Freddie to see a sex therapist next week. My doctor recommended this chap, a Mr Holmes, and I've been to see him already. He was very sympathetic and said that if I could get Freddie along and just talk about his problems, he would come to realise just why he's having all these troubles and could be reassured that basically he has nothing to worry about.'

Ivor and Beth wished the brave girl the very best of luck. Donna shook Freddie to wake him up and they moved away to where Brian Lipman was deep in conversation with Steve Elsey, the young photographer in whose honour the party was being held. But before they could join the two men, Paula sidled up behind them and tapped him on the shoulder.

'Here, come over in the corner, you two, I want to tell you something,' she whispered, and she dragged them off to the side of the room and went on: 'The boys have arranged a little surprise for Steve. Ken's hired a couple of working girls from Motherwell to come along and give him a send-off in style. Now the girls have just arrived and as soon as they're ready the lights will go out and the fun will begin.'

'Does Brian know about this?' wondered Ivor but

before Paula could answer him, there was a chorus of tiny screams and gasps as all the lights went out and the room was plunged into complete darkness. Then to his surprise, Ivor heard Brian gasp: 'Hey, what the hell's going on here?'

Above the noise of raucous laughter, there were sounds of scuffling and of clothes being ripped off. Then the pitch darkness in the room was relieved by a man who pulled out a torch from his pocket and shone a light directly onto Brian Lipman who was standing naked except for his underpants. He was flailing his arms against an attack by two equally nude girls who were obviously responsible for undressing him. One of the girls, a big-breasted redhead, now knelt in front of him and pulled down his pants. His circumcised cock sprang up and she grabbed hold of his rigid shaft and began to lick his helmet profusely before opening her mouth wide and taking in almost the whole length between her lips. At the same time, the other girl sat down underneath him and started to suck his balls.

To the cheers of the spectators, the girls made Brian lie down on the floor and the big-breasted girl mounted his throbbing erection and the second girl crouched over his face and urged him to lick out her pussy. The two girls faced each other and they kissed each other, caressing each other's breasts whilst the redhead rode Brian's cock and the other was being reamed out by his tongue and fingers.

But Ken Barret now pushed his way to the front of the watching crowd and yelled at the girls: 'Gail, Margie, you daft twats, that's the wrong man.

The girls looked up and Beth Rokeby's brother gesticulated violently and shouted: 'That's someone else! Steve Elsey is the tall fair-haired guy in the corner!'

Everyone roared with laughter as they realised that Gail and Margie were fucking the wrong man! 'Sorry about that, love,' said the redheaded Gail as she jumped off Brian's quivering prick. 'Yes, terribly sorry, Jimmy,' echoed Margie as she scrambled up and followed her friend who was already making a bee-line for Steve Elsey. 'Especially as you're a good pussy eater, whoever you are.'

Two guests held Steve by the arms and his struggles were to no avail as the girls pounced upon him. Paula took pity on Brian who was now standing crestfallen and alone. He bent down to slip on his pants but Paula went across to comfort him. She grasped his thick prick in her hand and said: 'Oh, poor old Brian! I shouldn't think you know if you're coming or going! Let me finish off where those rude girls left off.'

She knelt down in front of him and, curling her fingers around his swelling shaft, she licked and lapped around his helmet until his shaft was rock hard and then she gobbled it greedily into her mouth. She sucked lustily away and Ivor, who had glanced round from watching Steve Elsey being undressed by Gail and Margie, saw Paula's head bob to and fro as her lips moved rhythmically back and forth along Brian's veiny shaft whilst her gentle fingers stroked and tickled his balls.

Coupled with the previous efforts of Gail and Margie, this was too much for Brian to bear and with an almighty groan he took her tousled head in his hands and with a final shout of ecstasy, held her tight as his throbbing tool spurted out a frothy fountain of white seed into her throat. Paula milked his cock with enthusiasm, gulping down all his sticky jism until he withdrew his shrunken shaft from between her lips.

Meanwhile, Steve Elsey and the two girls were making

up for lost time. He was standing naked with his erect, pulsing prick being held tightly by Margie whilst Ken Barret and another journalist handed Gail a couple of soft cushions. She then lay down on the carpet with her head resting on one and the other underneath her bottom. She spread her legs and gave Steve a bird's eye view of her curly red bush as she toyed with her pussy, running her fingers along her crack as she crooned: 'Come on, Steve, I want you to screw me with that big cock of yours – don't be shy, my cunny is sopping wet and waiting for you.'

He hesitated a moment, but then Margie took hold of his straining shaft in her hand. With a yelp, Steve was pulled down to his knees. Margie placed the bulbous knob of his cock between Gail's yielding pussy lips and now he crashed forward, burying his delighted stiffstander into the depths of her juicy cunt. The girl wriggled and squirmed under his slim, athletic body and she worked her hips in conjunction with his eager thrusts, letting his throbbing shaft sink all the way inside her cunny channel, holding it there momentarily before he eased his glistening boner out to thrust forward yet again.

With barely a pause to take breath, Steve now began his final run-in to the winning post. Faster and faster he pistoned in and out of her pussy and with one last lunge forward, he let out a hoarse cry of triumph and ejaculated a stream of creamy jism into her eager snatch before collapsing down on top of her to the cheers of the excited audience.

But Margie placed her hands on her hips and called out: 'Well, is Steve the only red-blooded man here? Come on, isn't there anyone who'd like to fuck my nice tight pussy?'

There was a buzz of excitement and someone shouted out: 'Give Wayne a go!' To wild applause, a fresh-faced young teenage lad was dragged forward. Gail looked at him with amusement as he tried to plunge back into the crowd. Ken told her that Wayne was an office boy at the *Evening Express* and that tomorrow was his seventeenth birthday.

'And he's never been laid,' someone shouted and Margie clapped a hand to her face in horror. 'Never been laid? Oh, that's terrible, we can't have that, can we – come over here, pet, don't be shy.'

Steve now dragged himself to his feet and picking up his discarded clothes, went to dress himself in the same corner of the room which Brian Lipman had used. This allowed Gail to sit up and move over to where Wayne was standing, red-faced but with a bulge in his trousers which poked out like a pole between his legs. It was just as well that Donna had taken Freddie home for after the girls had stripped the birthday boy, the journalist would have been even further depressed at the sight of Wayne's enormous young prick.

'You could hang a week's washing out on that,' said Margie, clasping Wayne's cock and rubbing her hand up and down the blue veined shaft with professional skill. 'M'mm, it's certainly time it was put to good use.'

Still clutching his giant prick, she took Gail's place on the floor. Wayne paled when she spread her legs, but he was eager to take this opportunity of crossing the Rubicon. Margie guided him home and the lad trembled as he pushed through into her warm, clinging cunny until his balls swished against her raised bum cheeks. She crossed her legs and there was a hushed silence as the party guests watched the pair lie still for a moment before she heaved up her backside and he responded with a mighty shove of his own. And then they were off, and Wayne's sturdy young staff gleamed with her love juices as it jerked in and out of her clinging sheath in a furious rhythm. Of course, he came too quickly for her to achieve any great pleasure although Margie was thrilled to have taken the young man's cherry.

The guests clapped Wayne on the back as he gathered his clothes and joined Steve in the corner of the room which was now being used as an improvised dressing room. When Gail and Margie called for another volunteer, Beth looked at Ivor and murmured: 'I think it's going to be downhill all the way from now on. Would you mind very much if we left now?'

'Not in the slightest,' replied Ivor instantly. 'But first let me have a quick word with Brian and Paula, I'm sure they'd like to share our taxi.'

As he had correctly forecast, his colleague was equally keen to leave and whilst Beth's brother was being undressed by Gail and Margie to the raucous applause of the other guests, the four of them made a swift exit from the flat. Outside, light rain was falling but Brian Lipman soon spotted a man paying his taxi fare on the other side of the street and he sprinted across the road and reserved the cab for them.

Brian collected the keys of their rooms, and there was little problem smuggling in the girls after Ivor had slipped a crisp new five pound note into the gnarled hand of the night porter.

Upstairs, the two couples paired off and after saying good night to Paula and Brian, Beth stood outside Ivor's bedroom and waited for him to unlock the door. However, it was only at this moment that Ivor suddenly remembered that in all probability Chrissie and Tony Godfrey were probably still in his bed. He gnawed his bottom lip and then whispered to Beth: 'Oh dear, this is terribly embarrassing, Beth, but I should have mentioned that just as I was leaving the hotel tonight, I bumped into a chap I know named Tony Godfrey who you might have read about in the papers.'

'Tony Godfrey?' she said, raising her eyebrows. 'Tony Godfrey, now why is that name so familiar? Oh yes, of course, he's the man who gave ten thousand pounds for a signed Rolling Stones LP at that celebrity charity auction last month. He's a friend of yours, is he?'

'More of an acquaintance than a friend,' confessed Ivor and he hastily rearranged the facts as he went on: 'We had a couple of drinks with him and a girl he'd met in the bar. Well, to cut a long story short, he pulled me aside and said that he wanted to book a room here tonight for himself and the girl but the hotel was full. So I said they could use my room but I quite forgot to tell them to be out by midnight or whatever and so it's possible that they're still in there.'

'Well, can't we just go in quietly? If they've gone, there's no problem and if they're still there, we'll wake them up and they'll have to leave. It's very careless of you to have put us in this situation. However, I wouldn't mind meeting this Tony Godfrey character. He's always in the papers and seems to know everybody from the Prince of Wales to Elizabeth Taylor. I bet he could tell us a tale or two.'

'I'm sure he could,' agreed a much relieved Ivor as he inserted the key into the lock and slowly turned the door handle. He put a finger to his lips and pushed open the door just enough for Beth and himself to squeeze through into the short corridor on one side of which were cupboards and on the other, the entrance to the bathroom and toilet. Although they had switched off the main lights, Tony and Chrissie had left on the wall lights in the bedroom and Ivor and Beth could see their glistening nude bodies sprawled out on top of the rumpled sheets.

They were both awake and talking softly to each other. They did not hear their visitors come in and Ivor swallowed hard as he stared upon Chrissie's luxuriant blonde tresses which trailed down to the luscious curves of her breasts. He drew a sharp intake of breath as he gazed upon the golden fluff between her legs.

Ivor cleared his throat. 'Hello, there, folks. Sorry to have disturbed you, but I thought you'd be in the Land of Nod by now.'

'Hiya, Ivor,' said Chrissie, who moved herself slightly upwards to make herself more comfortable as she pressed her body against Tony's well-covered frame, although she made no attempt to conceal her delicious nakedness. 'No, we were just talking, or rather Tony was talking and I was listening to him.

'He's a great *raconteur* as well as being a very good fuck,' she added, as she lazily stretched out her hand and ringed her fingers round Tony's limp shaft. 'Now who's the pretty lady standing beside you? I hope she's not the hotel 'tec.'

'Let me introduce you,' said Ivor hastily. 'Tony and Chrissie, I'd like you to meet Beth, and no, she doesn't work for the hotel. Beth breeds pedigree labradors and she supplied the animals for our dog food promotion this morning.'

'Oh, I'm sorry, no offence meant,' apologised Chrissie. 'Ivor, why don't you and Beth have a glass of wine whilst Tony finishes his story. There's a half-full bottle of Chardonnay in the mini-bar. And I'll have one too whilst you're about it. How about you, Tony, would you like a refill?'

Tony Godfrey sat up and after gently moving Chrissie to one side, he hauled the eiderdown over their legs so that only Chrissie's jutting nipples were on display.

'Thanks, I'd love one,' he said, holding out his glass which Beth took from him and passed to Ivor.

Beth sat on the bed and said: 'I've read about you in the papers, Tony. If half of what they write is true, you must have had an interesting life.'

'I'm glad you don't believe everything you read in the papers,' he said wryly. 'Though I can't complain too much about what's been written about me. I am a lucky bugger as I've more than enough money thanks to dear old Dad's trust fund. It chokes the old boy to see me lazing àround and he can't threaten to cut me off without a penny, but years ago he had the choice of paying a hell of a lot of income tax or setting up a trust fund for my benefit, and he chose to keep the loot in the family.

'But I can't just sit around doing nothing all day, although you wouldn't think so from reading about me in the papers. I'm lucky enough to have money coming out my bum, as Chrissie put it earlier in the evening –' and he paused to give the girl a loving squeeze before he continued: 'and I don't see the point of letting it sit in the bank. Some people might call it an indulgence but I'm one of the biggest angels in the West End, if I say so myself.'

'What the heck's an angel?' asked Beth and Ivor explained as he brought over the drinks. 'An angel is someone who backs new plays. It costs a fortune to put on a show these days and there's always a struggle to find private investors like Tony to bankroll any new big productions.'

'Perhaps it's an indulgence but at least I'm providing employment,' Tony went on. 'Though I've backed a few winners, I'd be better off stashing the cash in the building society, though it would be a lot less fun.'

'Especially when you get to pick the chorus girls at the auditions!' joked Ivor with a grin but Tony was quick to deny the charge. 'If there is a casting couch, I never get the opportunity to lie on it,' he said, shaking his head. 'All I get apart from a share of any profits is two seats at the first night and an invitation to the party afterwards.

'Also, I sit on the boards of several charities and I raise money by organising concerts and other showbiz events for them.'

'You've met all the stars, haven't you? What was Elizabeth Taylor like when you talked to her at the party after the premiere of *Cleopatra*?'

'She was absolutely charming,' said Tony. 'And in my experience, the more famous the actor, the nicer the person. Oh, there are exceptions to the rule, of course, but I've never had the slightest hassle with the Hollywood stars, perhaps because they've made it and don't need to prove themselves any more. Treat them with the courtesy they're entitled to expect and you'll have no trouble with them. No, the people who can cause grief are strictly from division two – like the smart young comedian or pop star, the former film actress now in a TV soap opera. They're the ones who'll complain about your arrangements. They'll want cash in hand to speak at a charity dinner and ask for ten free tickets on top. Then they'll complain that the car you sent round to pick them up isn't big enough – well, you have some showbiz accounts, Ivor, don't you agree?'

'Yes, I do,' said Ivor, sitting down next to Beth on the edge of the bed. 'Take our biggest star, Ruff Trayde. You should see some of the letters he gets, they'd be enough to turn anyone's head, and they're not just from fifteen-year-old schoolgirls either! But in private, Ruff's the nicest chap you could ever wish to meet.'

'Isn't he supposed to be a shirtlifter?' enquired Chrissie. This brought an instant (if totally untrue) denial from Ivor, whose job was to project a macho image for the slightly built young man who, when not working, lived with a lorry driver at a secret address in the heart of the Cotswolds.

Chrissie snuggled closer to Tony and said: 'Just before you came in, I was asking Tony if he ever got lonely even with his mad rushing hither and thither. After all, unless the papers don't know about it, there doesn't seem to be a regular lady in your life.'

'There isn't one and I haven't been seeing anyone seriously for at least a year, which is just as well as I'm not ready yet to settle down.'

He pondered for a few moments and then continued: 'And it's true that I do sometimes feel lonely, even in a crowd of people. But as old Gilbert Harding once said to me, loneliness is simply a state of mind. For instance, I went out to Australia for a break a couple of years back with Benny Hill, who's an old mate of mine, and we were taken through the outback to a large cattle station. The rancher told me that his wife often packed a lunch for their kids and then sent them down to the river for a day by themselves. That way, he says, they'll learn the difference between solitude and loneliness.'

'I bet you're never short of a fuck, though,' said Chrissie roguishly and Tony raised his glass and said with a wink: 'You'd be surprised, my love. Why, this year alone there have actually been some weeks when I didn't have more than three different bed-mates.

'But it's a long time since I've had someone who makes love as well as you, Chrissie, that's for sure,' he added gallantly.

His reward for the easy compliment was a full-blooded kiss on the lips. 'Flattery will get you everywhere,' Chrissie giggled as she dived under the eiderdown to inspect his penis which, to her regret, remained disappointingly flaccid even whilst she slid her hand up and down his shaft.

'Sorry about that, Chrissie,' he said mournfully. 'I'd love to oblige but the old batteries need recharging.'

Beth suddenly perked up at these words and said: 'I've a good idea as to how that could be done!' She looked over to his curvy companion and said: 'Chrissie, I wonder if we could have a quick private word?'

'Of course,' replied the blonde girl and she slithered out of bed and followed Beth out into the bathroom.

'What's all that about?' asked Tony curiously but Ivor was equally puzzled. He shrugged his shoulders and replied: 'I've no idea, mate. Christ knows what they're planning in there, but I don't think you've got anything to worry about.'

Ivor and Tony strained their ears as they heard sounds of giggling from the bathroom. And when, a minute or so later, the girls returned arm in arm, the two men gaped at them. For Beth had undressed whilst she was in the bathroom and was now as nude as Chrissie.

'Move up, Tony,' ordered Chrissie gaily. 'If you're not up to making love yet, Beth has kindly volunteered to take your place.'

This did not displease the plump playboy who shifted himself across to the edge of the bed, allowing the two naked girls to fall into bed next to him in a tangle of arms and legs. Without further ado, they began to kiss each other, like sisters at first but then their kissing took on a fresh urgency and their mouths opened and Beth was sliding her hands up and down Chrissie's back until the blonde beauty was shuddering with desire, thrusting forward her quivering breasts against Beth's own soft body whilst Chrissie's hands moved down to squeeze the gorgeous round cheeks of Beth's bottom.

They continued to run their hands around each other with little squeals of delight. Beth pushed Chrissie onto her back and lay on top of her, tonguing her ear with rapid little flicks which brought deep purrs of contentment from the younger girl as she squeezed her legs together and murmured her encouragement.

Now past the point of any return, Beth ground her curly dark-haired pussy against Chrissie's flaxen muff and pressed the trembling girl's stiff, erect titties between her fingers. Then she substituted her tongue, drawing wet circles all round Chrissie's nipples before dipping her head downwards over her flat white belly towards her moist, silky nest. She planted a series of light, fluttery kisses all around Chrissie's honey-coloured bush before she carefully separated the soft folds of her cunny with her fingers and coaxed out the first dribblings of love juice from between her pouting pink love lips.

Chrissie moaned and writhed from side to side as Beth began to finger-fuck her in earnest and she opened her legs even wider. Meanwhile, both Ivor and Tony felt a familiar stirring in their groins as they gazed in awe at the red crack of Chrissie's cunny hole and of Beth's forefinger sliding in and out of her juicy slit.

'Ooh, I'm so wet, put more fingers inside me!' pleaded Chrissie and Beth immediately obliged, inserting a second and then a third digit inside her squelchy cunt, rubbing and playing with the gaping crimson slit, working her fingers in and out, faster and faster as Chrissie's cunny became wetter and wetter. She found the stiff little love button of her clitty and frigged it mercilessly with her thumb and forefinger whilst with the other hand she played with her hard, rubbery nipples, rubbing them fiercely against her palm. This made Chrissie shriek with delight and she spent profusely all over Beth's long fingers.

Ivor began to tear frantically at his clothes but Tony's naked prick was already in Chrissie's clutches. She lay on her tummy between his legs, nibbling and sucking his thick cock whilst Beth swung herself over his head, facing Chrissie. She closed her legs to trap Tony's head between her soft, warm thighs as he licked all along the edges of her love lips and clasped her gorgeous round bum cheeks in his hands.

'I'm going to suck you off, Beth,' Tony whispered passionately. 'Your juicy little quim will tingle like crazy before I'm finished with you. Do you like having a tongue sliding into your pussy? I'm going to lick you out, darling, starting right now . . .'

Beth squirmed her pussy even more firmly into his lapping tongue and mouth as Tony's lips closed around her dripping crack. With a maddening slowness, he pushed his tongue deep into the wet, tangy love hole, fondling the soft flaps of skin with his fingers.

By this time, Ivor had pulled off his clothes and he knelt next to the busy threesome, wondering how he could best join in this erotic frolic. He glanced down at Chrissie, who was fully occupied gorging herself on Tony's sinewy shaft. Ivor stood up and, carefully balancing himself with his legs straddling Tony's twitching torso, offered his prick for Beth to suck. The aroused girl eagerly leaned forward and Ivor gasped as she fondled his cock, peeling back the foreskin and tightening her grip as she kissed his bared knob. Then she crammed the throbbing tool into her mouth, drawing its soft fleshiness against her tongue until she felt it pulsing wildly at the back of her throat.

'A-a-a-h! A-a-a-h! A-a-a-h!' breathed Ivor as Beth dragged her tongue down to the base whilst she cuddled his hairy ballsack. His shaft jerked uncontrollably as she opened her mouth and let it go free, saying softly: 'It's all right, I won't stop but I don't want you to come too soon.'

Ivor closed his eyes as Beth gently squeezed his balls. She continued by rolling her tongue up into a tiny pointed arrow which circled round his smooth-skinned helmet. Then she raised her head slightly before powering her mouth down on the swollen crown of his cock, first simply holding it between her teeth and then running her tongue down the sides of the veiny shaft. She sucked slowly, tickling and working around the helmet whilst Tony continued to tongue her tingling cunny. Suddenly Beth straightened herself up and gasped: 'Oh my pussy's going wild, I must have some cock!'

With Tony Godfrey's pulsating prick still in her mouth, Chrissie looked up at her and opening her mouth she said: 'Okay, Beth, and how about swapping pricks to make it more interesting.'

'What a good idea,' said Beth and she hopped over to straddle Tony whilst Chrissie wriggled down between the two men and spread her legs, waiting to be fucked by Ivor's throbbing tool. She ran her hand across her fluffy blonde pussy hair and murmured: 'Oooh, I'm so wet, bang in your boner, Ivor, I need it really badly.'

Ivor leant himself gently over her and she pulled him down on top of her. Their bodies were glued against each other as their lips met in a burning kiss. Chrissie panted desperately into his mouth, her tongue quivering as if she were receiving an electric shock. She clawed at his back whilst he teased her sopping slit with the tip of his cock, rubbing it all along the edges of her gaping gash. And then, with a deep growl, he plunged his prick between the pouting red cunny lips and thrust his swollen shaft deep inside her welcoming love sheath. He fucked the gorgeous girl with powerful, sweeping strokes and Chrissie moaned with delight as his sinewy thick shaft swished to and fro, entering and re-entering her welcoming wet crack. She lifted her legs higher and wrapped her legs around his waist as they rocked together, faster and faster, in perfect rhythm. Chrissie let out an uninhibited yell of ecstasy as she climaxed and a small torrent of love juice flowed out of her pussy.

Now it was Ivor's turn to tremble all over as, with one almighty thrust, he slammed his shaft one last time into her squelchy love channel. His hoarse cry signalled his own orgasm as a flood of hot, sticky spunk washed the walls of Chrissie's cunny which set the happy girl off on a journey to a second blissful peak of pleasure.

Meanwhile, as they lay panting with exhaustion, Beth was kneeling on all fours, her beautiful bottom pushed out provocatively, her legs slightly apart, waiting for Tony to mount her doggie-style. But Tony was perspiring heavily as he slicked his hand up and down his semi-erect shaft. But when Chrissie saw that he was having a problem – caused by apprehension which fed upon itself when he penis initially failed to harden to peak erectness, as he later remarked – she slithered across under his thighs and began a lusty sucking of his hairy ballsack. Within seconds, this sensuous tonguing had the desired effect and Tony's tool soon stiffened to a rock-hard stiffness and was ready for work. He climbed into position as Chrissie now took hold of Beth's bum cheeks and pulled them apart, leaving Tony free to slide his thick prick through the narrow crevice between her buttocks and directly into her waiting wet cunt.

Beth tossed her head from side to side as his sinewy shaft pumped in and out of her juicy pussy. 'Faster, and harder!' she commanded and, nothing loath, Tony grabbed her hips and began pounding into her. But as her body gyrated wildly, his shaft slipped out of her cunny. And yet when Beth reached round and grabbed his knob, which had been well greased with her cuntal juices, she did not replace it between her pussy lips. Instead she moved it upwards against the wrinkled little entrance to her arse-hole.

Tony hesitated for a moment or two, but then he gingerly pushed forward into the tight-fitting orifice. Soon Beth was responding to every shove as he engineered four full inches of his cock inside her rear dimple. His balls bounced against the deliciously soft rounded cheeks of her backside as he moved in a fast-paced regular rhythm, back and forth, back and forth, snaking his hand round her waist and sliding his fingers through her luxuriant, crisp pussy hair and then rubbing his fingertips against her yielding cunny lips.

'Ooooh! Ooooh! Ooooh!' she screamed out and when, for a second time, Chrissie ducked her head underneath Tony and started to suck his balls, Beth's luscious bum cheeks wriggled joyously as he drove even deeper whilst he frigged her cunt.

'I'm going to shoot,' bellowed Tony and she yelled back: 'Yes, go on, empty your balls NOW!' and with perfect timing he lubricated her back passage with wodges of frothy white jism in a thrilling mutual climax. Ivor and Chrissie hailed this magnificent bum fuck with a spontaneous round of applause and the randy pair collapsed down with Tony's cock still enclasped inside Beth's bottom. Ivor helped Tony lift himself off Beth and the wealthy playboy grunted his thanks as he rolled off the bed and he blew Beth a kiss, saying: 'Whew, that was wonderful, but I'm absolutely drenched with sweat. Will you all excuse me while I have a shower?'

'I'll join you,' said Ivor, clambering over Chrissie to him. 'But I'm surprised at you, Tony, for talking in that way. My old English teacher at school always reminded us that horses sweat, men perspire and ladies glow!'

Tony chuckled and said to Ivor as they went into the bathroom: 'I didn't know you were educated at a posh public school, Ivor. Which one was it, Eton, Harrow or Winchester?'

'Webbs College, Wimbledon, as it happens, which is a jolly good state comprehensive. About seventy per cent of the kids passed four or more O-levels and about thirty per cent of the sixth form went on to University,' said Ivor proudly.

'Probably a darned sight better school than mine,' commented Tony as he switched on the taps. 'I was no great shakes academically – well, I was a lazy little sod, if truth be told – and so my parents packed me off to a posh and very expensive boarding school in deepest Gloucestershire.

'You wouldn't be talking of Osbourne Academy, by any chance?' said Ivor and Tony nodded as he climbed into the shower stall. 'Bloody hell, there's a coincidence, my cousin Marcus was sent there. Perhaps you knew him, Tony, Marcus Harcourt-Headleigh, he's about your age.'

'Mark Harcourt-Headleigh?' called out Tony. 'Yes, of course I remember him well, Mark Double-H we used to call him. Nice enough chap, bit on the quiet side, kept himself to himself and didn't make too many friends. Mind you, when we were both in the fifth form, there was a rumour that he was one of the boys who became involved with the gym master, if you follow my drift.

'It was only a rumour, I hasten to add, although they sacked the gym master shortly afterwards when they

139

caught him photographing a couple of boys fiddling with each other in the changing room. There was quite a bit of that going on between the prefects and the kids who had to run errands for them. At least you had the benefit of mixing with girls and had the opportunity of growing out of circle jerks and the like.'

Tony drew back the curtain and Ivor passed him a towel. 'Thanks, you can go in now. So what's happened to old Mark?'

'He's an editor for a small educational publisher. I believe he specialises in preparing maths and science textbooks. To be honest, I don't see very much of him. He's a quiet sort of chap, although the last time I saw him was when we bumped into each other in a restaurant and he had a very sexy-looking lady on his arm.'

'Good for Mark, I'm glad he didn't finish up limp-wristed. The story about the gym-master was probably just a rumour,' said Tony whilst Ivor took his place in the shower stall and turned on the taps. 'I don't want you to think we were all a bunch of pansies at school, far from it. But the problem was that most of us just never had the opportunity of meeting any girls.'

'I can't believe that you didn't find a way, Tony,' said Ivor who noticed with interest that the shower had been installed by Jetstream, the company he was going to see in a couple of days time.

Tony let out a small grunt of thanks as he rotated his body under the fierce jet of warm water. 'Nice of you to say so, old boy,' he said with a sigh. 'But I had to wait till I was almost seventeen and a half before I lost my cherry.'

Ivor came out of the shower and after drying his face on the last clean towel, replied: 'Well, so was I, and frankly, I don't think many fellows reached the winning post much earlier.'

'Maybe not, but at least you had some previous experiences – even if we're only talking about a fumble inside a blouse which is more than I ever managed. Remember, there weren't any girls at school and when I came home in the holidays, I had to rely on a couple of old pals I'd kept in touch with who hadn't gone to boarding school, to ask their girl friends to bring along someone to go out on a blind date with me. Believe it or not, Ivor, it took me a long time to gain any confidence with women.'

'Oh, I believe it all right,' said Ivor with a grin. 'There's nothing so awkward as those dreadful mid-teens, you remember, when you're more than a boy but not yet a man.

'Anyhow, with all these problems, I suppose you had to go to Soho on a Saturday night for your first fuck.'

'Not exactly, although that idea often crossed my mind,' admitted Tony as he reached up on the shelf for the talcum powder. 'No, the great event happened two days before the end of the spring term. My class had the afternoon off and most of the fellows went off with a couple of masters to a county cricket match at Cheltenham. But five of us decided to stay behind and play tennis instead. I played for the first hour but then I pulled a muscle in my back and the chap who'd been umpiring the game took my place as I limped off the court. I wasn't in that much pain and could have played on at a pinch, but it was a very warm day and truthfully, I'd had enough exercise, thank you very much.

'I went back alone to the changing rooms, stripped off and went through to the washroom to freshen up. Someone was already taking a shower and I glanced across to see if it was anyone I knew as I walked by. There weren't any curtains across the cubicles, of course, but the person rubbing soap across his face had his back to me.

'"Hi, who's there?" I called out and as the words left my lips, I realised that the shape of whoever was in the shower had long hair coming down to the middle of the back. As I took a closer look, I saw a body that had curves in very different places from me and the other boys in the History Sixth!

'My jaw dropped and I stood open-mouthed as, with a high-pitched yelp, this strange figure turned round. For the very first time I looked upon the beautiful body of a naked young girl. What had happened was that I had interrupted Lorraine, the eighteen-year-old daughter of the school gardener and handyman, who had been helping her father do something or other. Thinking that no-one would be about till lessons ended at four o'clock, she had decided to cool off with a nice refreshing shower.

'I stood transfixed and I gazed for the first time at a pretty girl's bare breasts. And what exquisite breasts they were – firm, white and rounded with large circled areolae topped with long, dark nipples!

'Lorraine had shaken off the water from her face and snatched a towel to cover her nakedness before she noticed me. I was standing as still as a waxwork, looking with a mixture of awe and excitement at the bushy growth of curly brown hair between her legs and the moist, glistening crack of her pussy.

'She looked with amusement at me and, dropping the towel, she said: "Well, well, it's Tony Godfrey, do you like what you see or would you like to have the merchandise wrapped up and sent back to where it came from, h'mm?"

'"No, I prefer to see the unwrapped goods, thank you," I said in a voice which cracked with emotion.

'She laughed and replied: "Yes, and from the way your cock's swelling up, I can see that you're telling the truth!"

'My face turned crimson when I looked down upon my

erect member which was standing up proudly against my belly. In the heat of the moment, I'd quite forgotten that I was as naked as Lorraine, who now stepped forward and stood directly in front of me. "My, my, that's a really massive shaft you've got down there, I bet it's the biggest truncheon in the lower sixth," she said approvingly. I almost fainted with excitement when she reached out and cupped my cock in her hands. She moved even closer and murmured: "Tell me the truth, now, Tony, has this thick prick of yours ever been inside a juicy wet pussy?"

'Still dumbfounded by what was taking place, I simply shook my head and Lorraine's eyes sparkled. "Well, don't you think it's high time that you did something about it?" she said softly and she pulled me by my rigid rod towards the baths. Still holding my throbbing tool in one hand, with the other she switched on the taps. Whilst the bath was filling up, she sank to her knees and began swirling her tongue around the top of my cock as she fondled my balls.

'At last I found my voice. "I'm going to come if you don't stop doing that," I warned, but Lorraine just gave a little nod and continued washing my helmet. When she jiggled the tip of her tongue on the underside of my knob, I couldn't hold back and I shot off inside her mouth.

'It shows how little I knew about sex that I was terrified by what we'd done. I was amazed that Lorraine gulped down my jism with every appearance of enjoyment. She saw the look of horror on my face and after switching off the bath taps, she said: "What's the matter, Tony? Didn't you like being sucked off?"

'"I loved it, Lorraine, but, er, I, um, well –" I mumbled and she let out a throaty little chuckle. "You're not worried that I'll get into trouble from swallowing your spunk, are you? It's one of the plus points about oral sex, you can't get pregnant from it! Anyway, it's your lucky day, Tony Godfrey, because you can fuck my pussy and spunk inside me as I'm on the pill!"

'Without further ado, she stepped into the bath and, still holding my now semi-stiff shaft as if her life depended on it, she invited me join her in the warm water. We soaped each other down and then Lorraine pulled out the plug. Only when the water had seeped out did she release my prick, which had now hardened up again to full erection.

'She pointed to her pouting pussy lips and said: "Now, Tony, lie on top of me and slip the tip of your cock inside my crack." I slithered down and tried frantically to push home my boner but everything was so slippery that I couldn't find the target. I let out a cry of frustration but Lorraine grabbed hold of my truncheon and slid my knob inside her juicy cunt. Oh, how marvellous it felt and I began to thrust away like a ram that had just cornered an elusive ewe. Of course, I came too quickly and in no time at all I jetted a torrent of jism inside her cunny.

'Lorraine lay still with a smile on her face as I scrambled out of the bath. At the time I didn't understand why she didn't follow me as I didn't realise that she hadn't climaxed. I wondered what she was doing as she continued to lie there with her eyes closed, frigging herself for all she was worth until she shuddered all over as she brought herself off.

'Well, although I had crossed the Rubicon, somehow I knew that I still had much to learn about the techniques of fucking. I said as much to Lorraine. "You did very well for a beginner," she said kindly, but she promised that the next time she would teach me more about love-making.

'That next time couldn't come too soon as far as I was concerned! We arranged to meet in my study later that evening after lights-out. I crept out of the dormitory and Lorraine was waiting for me there. We locked the door and began to snog passionately in the armchair. She took off her top and in the bright moonlight coming in through the window, I could see she wasn't wearing anything underneath it. Our tongues played frantically in each other's mouths whilst I rubbed and squeezed those gorgeous bare breasts. She pulled out my stiff prick from the slit in my pyjamas and slicked her hand up and down my tadger before she pulled her lips away and dived down to kiss my cock.

'Christ, I was lucky that no-one was around to hear me groan with ecstasy as she twirled her tongue around my shaft. But almost immediately she wriggled out of my arms, unzipped her skirt and pulled it down to the floor. Then she peeled off her brief white panties and stood stark naked in front of me, enjoying to the full the way I goggled at her superb nude beauty.

'She caressed her own pointed breasts and then she climbed over me, kneeling on the arms of the chair so that her cool white belly was inches from my face, and said: "Now it's time that you learned how to eat pussy, Tony. If you can perform well at this, you'll never have a shortage of girls willing to share your bed."

'I knew what was required of me though I was more than a little apprehensive as I kissed the soft skin of her tummy and then ran my lips lower into her silky brown thatch of curls. Nothing ventured, nothing gained, I thought, as I clasped hold of her glorious bum cheeks and drew her even closer to me as I buried my head between her thighs.

'Hesitantly, I started to lick around the edges of her pretty crack which was nice and moist. It took a little while to appreciate the pungent aroma which wafted out of her cunny but once I got used to it, I began to enjoy the experience, and from the way she ground her pussy against my face, I knew that I was doing well. Then remembering what I had read in *La Vie Parisienne* which one of my classmates had smuggled into the school, I moved my lips down the smooth-skinned creases of her cunt and lapped at her pouting love lips which slid open under the probing over my tongue. By chance, I found her clitty almost at once.

'Lorraine gasped as I nibbled away at the magic love button and began rolling my tongue around it. "Aaaah! Aaaah! Aaaah!" she breathed. "Well done, Tony, you're a natural pussy-eater – now be a good boy and bring me off with your fingers."

'Her praise gave me the confidence to prise open her love lips with my forefinger and I sank it deep inside her wet hole, making her tremble as I eased in a second and third finger. I didn't have to finger-fuck her for very long before she came all over my face, and I licked her out, swallowing as much of her tangy love juice as I could, which made her wild for another bout with my cock.

'I won't bore you with the details but I fucked her three more times before I crept back to the dormitory. I hadn't been missed but the next morning I was horrified to discover a large damp stain on my armchair! God, what would I say to the housekeeper, Mrs Newberry, if she questioned me about it? The bell rang for the first lesson of the day and I threw a sheaf of essay papers on the chair and prayed that Mrs Newberry or whichever of her two assistants was going to tidy my study, would not disturb the pile.'

Tony finished his story with a flourish and finished his glass of wine whilst Ivor, who had finished drying himself, folded his towel neatly across the heated rail and remarked: 'And were your prayers answered, or did the housekeeper ask you to explain how you'd dampened the furniture?'

'No, I was questioned about it, but more to the point, Lorraine left the school three days later to spend summer camping in the south of France with a group of friends. I never had the opportunity to continue our tryst. And I don't mind telling you, Ivor, that it was near enough another year on, just after I'd left Osbourne's, till I got another sniff of pussy.'

Ivor stood up and gave him a gentle prod on his shoulder. 'Meanwhile, you haven't done so badly, even if you did make a late start,' he grinned. 'For Christ's sake, Tony, you've fucked more women than I've had hot dinners!

'Come on now, let's go back inside or the girls will complain that we're neglecting them.'

'Oh I'm sorry, it's my fault, but I can't help getting on my hobbyhorse about the lack of sex education in single-sex boarding schools,' said Tony apologetically. As they re-entered the bedroom where they saw straightaway that Chrissie and Beth had indeed got bored with waiting for their return. They were locked in a passionate embrace, kissing rapturously and thrusting their tongues inside each other's mouths. Beth was taking the lead and she was clasping Chrissie firmly round the waist with her left arm whilst with her right hand, she was frigging the blonde girl's cunt. Her fingers slid at speed in and out of Chrissie's thatch of damp golden hair.

Chrissie parted her legs even further and the two men looked on with growing interest as they noticed that the gorgeous girl's clitty was projecting out between her cunny lips. As if in unison, their cocks started to swell and harden as Chrissie cried out: 'Oh, I'm coming! I'm coming!' and they watched an arched fountain of love juice spurt out from between Chrissie's cunny lips as her body bucked and heaved whilst she enjoyed her delicious orgasm.

'Now let me finish you off,' she insisted, and it was Beth's turn to lie flat on her back with her legs opened wide, whilst Chrissie leaned over and began rubbing her fingertips along her crack. Beth moaned as Chrissie kissed her nipples and then rolled on top of her, pressing her face between her breasts as she eased her forefinger inside Beth's squelchy slit. Her thumb prodded the aroused clitty and Beth shivered with delight as Chrissie withdrew her finger and ran it wickedly down the full length of her crack.

'See, the parting of the ways,' said Tony cleverly. Ivor laughed as Chrissie swivelled herself between Beth's raised thighs. Her bottom wobbled high in the air as she started sucking Beth's sopping cunny, forcing her tongue deep inside her juicy love channel, which made her thresh wildly from side to side.

The two men glanced at each other and silently Ivor moved forward, his erection bobbing stiffly between his legs, and joined in the fun by positioning himself behind Chrissie and sliding his cock between her soft bum cheeks and into her dripping cunt.

'Well played, sir,' called out Tony Godfrey in the style of a well-known TV sports commentator. 'But as I said to the British snooker champion, can you tell our viewers if you're going for the pink or the brown?'

Ivor was too busy to answer but Tony was not that interested in his reply. Instead he lumbered to the side of the bed and presented his own throbbing erection to Beth, who turned her head and smothered his cock with kisses, fondling the hot, smooth-skinned shaft and rubbing it against her cheek. Then she popped her lips over the straining bared crown and sucked on it in frantic, slurping gulps.

At the same time, Chrissie continued to lap her juicy pussy and nibble on Beth's clitty which had burst out of its pod, quivering wildly as Chrissie nipped at the rubbery flesh with her teeth. And Chrissie herself was delighting in the electric currents of sheer bliss which were emanating from her pussy as Ivor relentlessly ploughed his prick in and out of the hungry love-hole.

Beth was the first to explode, rubbing herself off to a glorious orgasm against Chrissie's mouth. The blonde girl lifted her head and yelped with glee as Ivor creamed her cunny with a coating of sticky spunk as he ejaculated his sperm inside her. Chrissie reached up and took Tony's shaft in her fist, slicking her hands up and down his tool whilst Beth gobbled on his knob. Very soon, with a wrenching cry, he spurted his seed down Beth's throat. She swallowed all his jism, milking every last drain of cum from his trembling tool.

As the participants finished this four-handed fuck in a sticky tangle of nude bodies, Tony Godfrey gasped: 'Phew, that was a wonderful screw but I need a drink. Anyone care to join me? What'll it be – whisky, gin, brandy, we've a good selection in the mini-bar.'

'Truthfully, I'd prefer a nice cup of tea,' confessed Chrissie and Beth nodded her head and said: 'Good idea, pet, I'll have the same, please.'

'Make it three,' added Ivor quickly and Tony reached for the kettle and commented: 'Yes, why not? I'll have one too if I can find enough cups.

'There's nothing in the world to beat the drink that refreshes but does not inebriate,' he concluded in a fair imitation of W C Fields. He added another *bon mot* of the great American comedian. 'It sure beats what comes out of a tap – not that I'd drink water, fish fuck in it!'

As he went into the bathroom to fill the kettle, he called out: 'Actually, making tea after making love reminds me of a weird experience I had a few weeks ago in Huddersfield, of all places.'

'Huddersfield? Isn't that somewhere in the North of England?' asked Beth as she lazily smoothed her hand across Ivor's flaccid prick which lay dormant over his thigh.

'Yes, you must have heard of the old rhyme, Beth,' Ivor smirked as she squeezed his limp shaft. 'She was only a farmer's daughter but she liked her udders feeled! Ow! Don't pull my cock, you'll do me a mischief!'

'Serves you right telling such a dreadful joke, but play your cards right and I might kiss it better after tea,' she replied perkily.

Tony chuckled and said: 'Funnily enough, I was staying just south of Huddersfield near the famous village of Rokeby. Beth, your family doesn't come from round those parts, do they?'

'Rokeby's my ex-husband's name, but his family's from the Highlands,' she replied. 'But what's so special in this village?'

'Nothing much these days, but it gave its name to one of the world's most treasured paintings,' Tony explained as he sat on the bed. 'Do I take it then that none of you have heard of *The Rokeby Venus*?'

His three listeners looked blankly at him and Tony tut-tutted as he switched on the electric kettle: 'Dear, oh dear, let me fill this gap in your education. *The Rokeby Venus* is the name given to Velazquez's only painting of a female nude which hangs in the National Gallery in London. The painting's real name is *The Toilet of Venus* but it's always been known as *The Rokeby Venus* because its former owners lived in Rokeby.'

'Wait a minute, wasn't this one of the paintings slashed by the Suffragettes?' enquired Ivor, hazily recalling a lecture by a guide when he had allowed a girl friend to drag him round the National Gallery on a dull Sunday afternoon.

'Absolutely right, give that clever lad a toffee apple,' applauded Tony as he set out the cups and saucers. 'Damn, we're one cup short, Ivor. You and I will have to share.'

'That's alright with me, I don't think I can catch anything from you by drinking from the same cup! But come on, Tony, tell us about what happened to you in Yorkshire.'

'You cheeky bugger! Take no notice of him, girls, I'm a clean-living chap. Which brings me nicely to what happened during that weekend. I'd been invited up there by Paul Lumbsdon, an old chum of mine from college days. Paul's family owns great chunks of Yorkshire but he's not a gadabout and he and his wife Maureen live quietly with their young kids in this wonderful old country house miles from anywhere. I suppose Paul's a bit like me, he's got so much loot stashed away that he doesn't need to work, except to attend a board meeting every six months. Funny thing is, they're both avid Socialists and donated God knows how much to the Labour Party before the last election – which must have made Paul's old man turn in his grave.

'But that's by the by. The point is that Paul and Maureen give these marvellous weekend parties where you're always bound to meet a wide selection of interesting people. Well, this weekend I became friendly with a couple who lived at a nearby American air base,

Colonel and Mrs Carstairs. Now Woody Carstairs must be in his early forties but his wife, Yoko, was a beautiful Eurasian girl at least fifteen years younger than him, whom he'd met and married when he was serving in the Far East.

'There were three other guests, two women and another man, Richard what's his name, the Liberal MP for South Cornwall. Well, Maureen made a superb meal on the Saturday night for the eight of us and after dinner the men and women split up and we played bridge. I partnered Woody against Paul and we held the most terrific cards and it was just as well that we were only playing for ten bob a hundred. I think we bid and made two grand slams, both vulnerable, and when we reckoned up at the end, Woody and I had won twenty-four pounds each.

'Everyone else except Woody and I had drifted off to bed, but we were getting on famously, toasting our partnership at the card table with a bottle of Remy Martin. Then Yoko came into the room and I have to admit she looked very, very sexy indeed. Dressed only in silk pyjamas, she was beautiful by any standard with her sultry black eyes set in a pretty face, porcelain skin, small but rounded breasts and surprisingly long legs for such a little girl.

'"Will you be coming to bed soon?" she asked Woody politely and he told her that he'd join her upstairs in about another ten minutes. She bowed slightly and added meaningfully: "I'll have the tea ready when you do come up," as she closed the door behind her.

'Being naturally nosey, I wondered what was behind this cryptic remark and so I said to Woody: "Surely you don't want any tea after polishing off more than half of this bottle of brandy, old man."

'Woody chuckled as he threw his arm round my shoulders and said confidentially: "Oh yes I do, but not to drink!" He laughed out loud again and explained: "Between ourselves, I always took two spoons of sugar with my tea or coffee and Yoko was concerned that my sugar intake was too high. So she showed me a great way how to make tea taste sweet without adding a grain of sugar."

'To my amazement, he grabbed hold of my arm and went on: "Here, Tony, you come on up with me and you'll see for yourself what I mean. Don't worry, Yoko won't mind, she enjoys being watched whilst making love."

'I was now genuinely puzzled but *very* curious to find out what Woody had in mind. When we reached the Carstairs bedroom Woody said: "Wait here a minute, Tony, I'll call you in when we're ready." And I didn't have to wait long till I heard him shout: "Okay, come on in."'

Puffs of steam started to rise from the kettle and Tony switched it off. He popped four tea-bags into the tea-pot and filled it with boiling water.

'Did Woody call you in to offer you his wife?' asked Beth with interest. 'I thought this was a custom only amongst the Eskimos.'

'Not exactly,' Tony went on. 'I went in and saw Woody sitting cross-legged on the bed. He was naked and his cock was jutting upwards like an arrow ready to fly. Yoko was also naked but she was kneeling in front of him with the small white mounds of her rounded bottom pushed out towards him and she was calmly soaking her pussy with a sponge which she was dipping in and out of a pot of tea!

'Woody looked at me and explained: "You've heard of the Japanese tea ceremony! Well, this is much more fun!" He slapped Yoko lightly on her thigh and began massaging her buttocks. Then she moved backwards and slowly lowered her arse onto his thick shaft and his knob disappeared between those beautiful bum cheeks. At first I thought he was trying to enter via the tradesmen's entrance but when I moved round to the front of the bed to get a better look, I could see that he had slid his cock into her pussy.

'Yoko wriggled happily as Woody swung his arms round her and began to play with her nipples, rubbing them against the palms of his hands. She started sliding sensually up and down on his veiny stalk, faster and faster until I thought even his big hairy balls would be sucked up inside the crevice of her backside.

'He closed his eyes and growled and his body began to shake all over as Yoko rode him like a cowboy at a rodeo, opening and closing, clenching and unclenching those perfect bum cheeks, mewing and gasping until all of a sudden they shuddered together and their bodies went limp. Then when Yoko pulled herself off his shrivelled prick, she lay down next to Woody and he swung himself over between her legs and began to lick her juicy pussy. Yoko drummed her heels on the mattress in sheer ecstasy as he made her come again. Soon his cock was hard again and he scrambled over her and they threw themselves into another passionate fuck in the good old-fashioned missionary position.

Ivor said drily: 'I'd also like to cut down on sugar with tea or coffee, and I've got nothing against eating pussy – far from it – but your friend's substitution of love juices is interesting to say the least. But it's not very practical.

'For instance, I don't think I could get away with going downstairs for breakfast tomorrow morning and rogering the waitress when I wanted to drink my tea. Neither of us would have the time and it might put other people off their food.'

154

'Yes, and you'd have a problem if only waiters were on duty!' said Beth solemnly. They all burst out into peals of laughter as Tony poured out the tea and whilst he was handing round the cups, they were startled by a *tum, tiddley, om pom, pom pom* knocking on the door.

'Who can that be at this time of night?' asked Beth as she covered herself with a sheet.

Ivor slipped on his dressing gown and went to investigate. He opened the door slowly but turned his head round and called back to his guests: 'Relax, folks, it's only Paula and Brian.'

The new arrivals, also wrapped in dressing gowns, followed Ivor inside and Paula said: 'Oh, how funny, we've just had a cup of tea too. But poor old Brian had to have his without sugar as the chambermaid must have forgotten to put any out.' The girl looked at Brian with a puzzled expression as her listeners exploded into laughter.

'Well, what's so funny about that?' she demanded and Brian shrugged his shoulders and sniffed the air. 'Buggered if I know, love. Perhaps they've been smoking naughty cigarettes but I can't smell any evidence. All right then, folks, what's the joke?'

But this made the others laugh even more until Tony wiped his eyes and explained what they had been talking about just before Brian had knocked on the door.

'Well, I've heard of strange connections with food and sex but that is pretty weird,' commented Paula. 'Although I do know a girl who likes her man to rub a half-eaten banana smothered in raspberry jam all over her and have him lick it all off after she's gobbled down the banana.'

'Different strokes for different folks,' grunted Brian. Slipping off his dressing gown, he slid into bed next to

Chrissie as Ivor said sarcastically: 'Do make yourself at home, old man.'

'Thanks, Ivor, I will,' he replied, ignoring the irony in Ivor's tone as he snuggled up to Chrissie and said: 'Oooh, you're nice and warm, pet. Hey, Chrissie, you're not the girl Paula is talking about are you? I'm afraid I don't have a banana on me but I've something else shaped like one which I'll gladly dip in raspberry jam for you!'

She slid down her hand and squeezed his limp cock. 'Not much to get my mouth round there, I'm afraid! But no, I'm not really into that type of scene, although come to think of it, a couple of months ago I was inspired by a packet of instant mashed potato!'

'This we have to hear,' said Tony, plumping himself down next to Beth. 'Room for a small one?' asked Ivor and all six somehow managed to squeeze onto the double bed amidst much friendly shoving and giggling.

'Come on, Chrissie, spill the beans,' urged Paula, and Chrissie yelped as Brian slid his hand under her peachy bottom and repaid with interest her squeeze of his cock. 'It was mashed potato, not beans and I know it sounds silly but if you had been there, I'm sure you wouldn't have acted any differently.

'It's a small world, you know, because it all started when I went with a girl friend to a Ruff Trayde and the Trayders concert. Your firm handles their publicity, doesn't it, Ivor? Well, my friend Annabel and I went round backstage afterwards to get Ruff's autograph when he came out of the theatre.'

That's all any girl would get from Ruff, thought Ivor wearily. He wondered for how long he would be able to hoodwink the press and public about the deviant sexual preferences of the lithe young man who strutted the stage in tight leather trousers.

'I happened to catch the eye of one of Ruff's roadies, a slim, good-looking chap with twinkling blue eyes and a moustache. He came out from the stage door and told the crowd of girls that Ruff wouldn't be leaving for at least an hour, but that he'd collect autograph books to be signed and come back with them in five minutes.

'He was as good as his word but as he gave me mine back, he said: "Are you alone? Oh, just you and your friend, is it? Okay, well you two come with me." As he shepherded us through the stage door he said: "Ruff's getting changed and then he and the boys want to go through some work for tomorrow night's concert, but he'll just come out for a minute to meet you. Now, what are your names?'

'Don't tell me,' broke in Ivor. 'This must have been Tony Mulliken, Ruff's personal manager. He's a sucker for pretty blondes.' This made Brian snort: 'And aren't we all, for God's sake?'

Chrissie acknowledged Ivor's interruption. 'Yes, Tony introduced himself and then Ruff came out and signed our books personally. He's a quiet sort of guy in real life, so different to the impression he gives on-stage. We were very excited of course and then another broad-shouldered guy in jeans and short-sleeved shirt passed by and Tony pulled him over and introduced him to us. "This is Steven Williams, he's Ruff's road manager. Annabel, if you're interested in what goes on behind the stage, Steven will be pleased to explain everything to you."

'Of course, that was the last I heard from Annabel till the next morning. She said Steven was a great shag, but that's another story. It was getting late and I asked Tony: "Have you eaten anything tonight?" He shook his head and replied: "As a matter of fact, I haven't."

'I said: "Well it's too late to go to any decent restaurant,

157

so how about coming back to my place and I'll cook us both some dinner?" He looked a little taken aback at my boldness but then replied shyly: "That's real Scottish hospitality for you. Thanks, Chrissie, I'd love to. Hold on a minute and let me get something from my office." He returned with a bottle of red wine and said: "Steven and I were going to drink this with some sandwiches but he and Annabel are going back to the hotel coffee shop."

'I grilled two steaks and cooked some instant mashed potato and then afterwards we settled down on the sofa to finish the rest of the wine. Well, one thing led to another and after a while we were grappling away, french-kissing like mad whilst we undressed each other. Once Tony had helped me take off my blouse, he unhooked my bra and when it fell to the floor and he saw my bare breasts, he smiled wolfishly and finished undressing me whilst I unzipped his flies and pulled down his trousers.

'When we were both naked, the saucy monkey drew me down on the sofa and started to kiss my nipples. My God, he was good! The way he sucked and lapped round my titties alone almost brought me off! I swear that my boobs grew to the size of melons and my nips got all hard and wrinkly. Then just as I was going to ask him to lick me out, he dived between my thighs and put that magic tongue of his to even better use!

'I moaned as he slipped a finger into my cunny whilst he explored the folds of my love lips with the tip of his tongue. Suddenly he stopped and he picked up the wine bottle and poured a little of the red liquid right into my cunt! Then he leaned over and lapped it all up together with all my pussy juice in long, sensuous swallows. He made me come twice this way and then he sat up and then I left him sitting on the sofa whilst I dashed into the kitchen to find something that I could eat off his body.

'I found some ice-cream cones but we'd eaten all the ice-cream for our dessert – but then my eye fell upon the leftover mashed potato. I scooped up some in the cone and walked back to the sofa and Tony stood up with his big cock standing up in front of his tummy.

'"Oh no, what are you going to do with that," he chuckled, when he saw the ice-cream cone and he flinched, thinking that it was filled with cold ice-cream. But when I plunged the cone over his cock and he felt the thick, warm potato he sank back and sighed with pleasure. I smeared the gooey mess all over his shaft and massaged some over his balls. Then I licked off every last bit, like a cat, and he just adored it. By the time I'd worked my way up to his knob, he was gasping like crazy and clutching my hair and I knew he was going to shoot his load. So I took his knob between my lips and let it slide back down my throat. It took only a few seconds before Tony spunked and I swallowed all his sticky jism which nicely washed down all that mashed potato!'

Chrissie's story about Tony Mulliken had the effect of firing up his namesake, Tony Godfrey, who had moved himself to the end of the bed where he was lovingly sucking Paula's big toe. 'Now that's something that a lot of girls like but doesn't do very much for me,' exclaimed Beth as Brian gently caressed her breasts. 'I love to have a man play with my nipples but toe-jobs leave me cold.'

'Oh, you don't know what you're missing,' Paula panted as Tony ran his tongue up and down her toe. 'My feet are super-sensitive and Tony's turning me on almost as much as if he were playing with my pussy.'

'I like having my ear-lobe nibbled,' confessed Beth who was fortunately sandwiched between Ivor and Brian. They willingly obliged as she took each of their swelling cocks in her hands and slid her fingers up and down their hot, stiff shafts. Chrissie moved herself next to Tony at the other end of the bed and placed her soft, warm body between Beth's legs. She lovingly kissed her moist, hairy muff whilst Tony, whose mouth was busy sucking Paula's toe, slipped his hand inside the crevice between Chrissie's dimpled bum cheeks and ran his fingers around the edges of her own damp crack.

Beth slicked her hand up and down Ivor's shaft so sensuously that he came very quickly and immediately Beth transferred her sticky fingers to Brian's throbbing prick which she held in both hands as she leaned over and washed his knob with her tongue. At the same time, Paula called out for Tony to fuck her so he was forced to stop diddling Chrissie's cunny and climb on top of Paula and start pistoning his prick in and out of her juicy love channel.

With an agility which surprised even himself, Ivor swung himself over the heaving bodies and landed on his knees between the backs of Chrissie's parted legs. He slid his arm underneath her and pulled her gorgeous bottom up so that he could place his face underneath and lick at her blonde haired pussy from behind. He found her wet notch and stuck his tongue through the pouting love lips as Chrissie groaned with sheer delight.

Brian Lipman's eyes were closed and his head was thrown back in ecstasy as Beth sucked lustily on his iron-hard shaft. He let out a heartfelt sigh as she let her tongue flick around the red crown of his cock before drawing his shaft in between her rich, generous lips, sucking as hard as she could. Instinctively he arched his hips upward, fucking her mouth as her soft hands toyed with his heavy balls which were now tightening in their hairy sack.

Gently, Beth squeezed his balls and was rewarded by a fierce fountain of spunk which burst out of his knob and filled her mouth. Swallowing hard, she drained his quivering cock, nibbling daintily at his helmet until the last milky drops had been coaxed out of his softening member.

Paula was now on the verge of a climax and she squealed with happiness as Tony pistoned his thick prick, faster and faster, in and out of her squelchy cunny, keeping hold of her rounded buttocks in his hands as his body slewed first one way and then the other, his glistening cock emerging at every long plunging stroke before he thrust back inside her clinging, squelchy sheath.

With a gutteral cry, Tony jetted a fountain of frothy white seed deep inside her willing cunt. He was pleased to feel Paula's teeth sink into his shoulder as she also achieved a climax, just before Tony's throbbing tool began to deflate. He continued to pump away until he flopped off her and rolled over to her side, utterly exhausted by his vigorous efforts.

Beth now tightened her thighs around Chrissie's pretty head whilst the blonde girl finger fucked her and sucked her clitty until Beth came with a huge shudder and flooded Chrissie's mouth with her tangy cuntal juice. And Ivor placed the last piece in the sexual jig-saw by frigging Chrissie's cunt with his fingers from behind until she also spent and the six horny young people lay, quietly sated, until the first rays of dawn pierced the thin cotton curtains.

❀ FOUR... ❀

The Last Round-Up

Brian and Paula preferred to stay the rest of the night with their friends. Fortunately, a simple stratagem suggested by Tony Godfrey led to Chrissie, Ivor and himself being given pillows and sleeping at one end of the bed whilst the others slept on the other. It worked surprisingly well and they all managed to snatch a few hours sleep until the buzz of the alarm on Ivor's wrist-watch stirred him from his slumber.

Ivor glanced at his watch and saw that it was half past seven. He yawned and narrowly missed slamming his clenched fist into Tony's nose as he stretched out his arms. Then a mischievous thought suddenly struck him. Ivor grinned gleefully as he climbed carefully over the recumbent bodies of his sleeping companions, picked up the bedside telephone and dialled room service.

'Hello there, I'd like to have breakfast in my room, please. Sorry I didn't leave the card outside my door last night! But I don't need it brought up for another three quarters of an hour, that's at a quarter past eight. Will that be possible? It will? Oh, super, thank you very much.

'Continental or British? Oh, we'll have the works, please. Yes, I said we, but no I don't want two breakfasts,

I want six sent up to room two hundred and thirty seven.'
Ivor chuckled openly as he imagined the surprised face of
the girl who was taking down his order. Then he suddenly
reminded himself of Brian Lipman's dietary requirements
and went on: 'Yes, that's correct, six full breakfasts,
orange juice, cereal and tea for all but five with bacon and
egg and one with grilled kippers.'

Perhaps I've gone too far, he thought. I don't want
anyone snooping round to see who's been sleeping in my
room so he added: 'I'm holding an early morning meeting
up here with my colleagues so please be punctual and
have the food here at eight fifteen sharp. Thank you,
goodbye.'

He put down the phone and leaned across to kiss the tip
of Chrissie's nose. She opened her eyes and murmured:
'Hiya, lover,' before snuggling down again and continuing her sleep. Ivor squatted down on his haunches and
whispered in her ear: 'I hope you and Paula are on the
eleven o'clock shift again at Websters, Chrissie, because
it's already past half past seven.'

Chrissie sat up and rubbed her cheek. 'Yes, thank God
we don't have to be in at half past eight!' she replied
sleepily, but then she heaved herself up and sighed: 'But
there's no peace for the wicked. We still have to get home
and change before going to work. I'll have a quick shower
and then we'd better wake Paula. Any chance of a bite of
breakfast before we go?'

'I've ordered our breakfasts to be sent up here,' said
Ivor as he helped her struggle out of bed without waking
the others. 'Go on, love, you run your bath and I'll wake
up Paula in five minutes.'

In fact, Paula began to stir when Chrissie clambered
over her legs to get out of bed. 'What's the time, Ivor?'
she asked anxiously as she woke up and Ivor explained the

situation to her. 'Oh well, that's not too bad,' she said as she slipped out of bed, taking care not to disturb Tony, Brian and Beth who were still fast asleep. 'Chrissie's having a shower, is she? I'll have one too. Since her brother-in-law installed one in our flat, I don't take a bath very often.'

'Ah, I'm glad you mentioned Chrissie's brother in law, since I want to speak to him about his company's publicity,' said Ivor. Then he grimaced in frustration. 'Hell, my memory cells are dying, Paula, what's the chap's name? Chrissie did tell me but I've forgotten it.'

'Mike Lewis, he's a smashing guy and I'm sure you'll get on well with him,' she answered and Ivor said quickly: 'Tell me more about Mike. Chrissie made him sound like a whizz-kid to me.'

'Well, he's done very well since he left school at sixteen and started work for a wholesale warehouse, selling cheap booze to licensed grocers. Jetstream took him on as a junior representative in the West of Scotland four years ago and since then he's risen through the ranks. Six months ago he was made the sales manager for Scotland and Northern England. And right now he's the managing director's blue-eyed boy because last month he clinched a deal for Jetstream to supply and instal showers for that big new hotel being built in Edinburgh.'

'He must be a great salesman,' commented Ivor. Paula smiled and said: 'Oh, Mike's the best, he could sell sand to the Arabs. He's not one of the Flash Harry types though. He's a quiet, friendly sort of man, the sort that people know they can trust.'

'They often turn out to be the biggest villains,' said Ivor cynically but Paula defended her description. 'Maybe, but Mike plays by the rules,' she said with added emphasis. 'For instance, he used to have a reputation for being a ladies' man before he met Chrissie's sister but since they've been married Chrissie will tell you that Mike hasn't ever played away – even though we know there've been girls in his office who've been waving their knickers at him at company parties.'

'Good for him, there's enough competition for crumpet without married men cheating on their wives,' said Ivor, thinking of how Martin Reece was wining and dining his pretty young secretary in the absence of his wife, a renowned consultant pathologist who spent many days away from home at international medical conferences.

'Glad to hear you say that,' chimed in Chrissie as she came back from the bathroom. 'Most married men are bad news. Now did I hear you two talking about Mike?'

'Yes, I'd be very grateful if you could help me fix up a meeting with him, Chrissie. I think he would be interested to see what my company could do publicity-wise for Jetstream Showers.'

Chrissie sat down on a chair and pulled on her panties. 'No problem, Ivor, I'll call him at his office after breakfast,' she said as Paula padded into the vacant bathroom. 'You know, it's true what Paula said about Mike, he doesn't play around at work and I wish that Paula would follow his example. She's having a fling with young Duggie Daley, our supervisor. Duggie's not married but he's got a regular girl friend and he and Paula only get it together during lunchtimes and tea breaks at work in the storeroom.'

'Well, why does she carry on with the affair?' said Ivor as he slipped on a dressing gown. Chrissie continued to dress herself as she replied: 'She just likes a good, simple fuck with no strings attached. But she should realise that the time's come to call it a day, and she and Jock should either start a proper relationship or stop screwing each other before someone gets hurt. Let's face it, in ninety-nine times out of a hundred, that will be the girl.'

Ivor's face coloured as he thought of past office liaisons which had, as Chrissie had said, ended in tears. He had sworn never to mix business with pleasure, although he didn't include the crowd of pretty models who could be constantly found in the nearby studio of Brian Lipman, who also considered entertaining the girls to be a perk of his profession.

'Mind, I'm a fine one to talk, because I recently had a thing going with Mr Webster,' she confessed.

'What, not old Willie Webster who founded the chain. He must be getting on for seventy!' said a shocked Ivor.

'No, no, this was Jack, his eldest son. It all started at last year's Christmas party which we held in a big pub not far from our branch. We'd all had a few drinks and Jack was telling me how he was missing his wife who was away for a few days visiting her parents who live down South near Leamington Spa. Anyhow, somehow the conversation got round to oral sex and Jack said how few men knew how to pleasure a woman properly with their lips. "You're quite right," I said to him. "My boy friend, Sandy, is very well endowed with a thick, meaty eight-inch cock but he doesn't know anything about oral sex and isn't at all keen to learn."'

Chrissie stepped into her dress and zipped it up as she continued: 'Jack asked me whether I minded missing out on oral sex and I answered truthfully that I used to adore having my pussy eaten, but it had been so long ago since anyone had licked me out that I'd almost forgotten how much I liked it. "Well, let's do something about that tonight," he said and I agreed to slip away with him just before the party was due to finish.

'He drove me to his big house in Newton Mearns and

the next thing I knew, we were lying naked on the bed and he was going down on me. After he brought me off we got into a sixty-nine and I sucked his cock. It was only half the size of Sandy's but it tasted just as nice whilst he was busy eating me out and we were both loving it.

'Then he asked me to mount him and, as I rather enjoy being on top, I didn't need to be asked twice. I lowered my wet pussy over his rock-hard tadger and bounced up and down on it whilst he played with my titties. Almost immediately he came in a tidal rush of hot spunk but he managed to keep his sturdy prick stiff till I climaxed and slumped down across him.

'He wanted me to stay but I suddenly realised that I'd arranged to meet Sandy. So he drove me home and I only had time to wash my hands and face before Sandy arrived. Now I don't know whether it was the sparkle in my eyes or my flushed complexion which I usually have after a good fuck, or whether Sandy was just feeling exceptionally horny! But he practically tore off my clothes as soon as he came in and began ramming his huge cock into me. And do you know something, Ivor, his prick felt even better than ever but thank God he never realised why my cunt was so well lubricated! He just said how much he loved it when my pussy was all wet and juicy because he could fuck me quickly and easily when it was that way.

'This happened again a few times and Sandy never found out that my pussy was still wet because another cock had been reaming me out before he slid his thick tool inside my cunt. I really enjoyed having both Jack and Sandy on the same day, preferably as close to each other as possible, but it was just as well that old Mr Webster sent Jack to America for a month to study supermarket operations out there, and the affair died of its own accord.

'Sandy and I also called it a day as we could both see

that we were going nowhere, but we're still friends – though of course we don't fuck each other any more. I do miss his giant prick now and then, but then size isn't everything, which is just as well or you'd be in a lot of trouble, wouldn't you, Ivor?' she finished teasingly.

Ivor looked at her with a pained expression. 'Just for that, I'm going to put Percy away for the day,' he said in mock affront. Chrissie slid her hand between the folds of his dressing gown and, as she grabbed hold of his cock, she giggled: 'Now, now, don't sulk, I was only joking, you've got a lovely cock which fills my pussy beautifully.

'And my mouth too,' added Chrissie as she clenched her fingers round his swelling shaft and slicked her fist up and down until he was fully erect. Then she dropped to her knees and planted a full, moist kiss upon the bared helmet.

'There, that's better,' she cooed as Paula came back from the bathroom. Without hesitation she joined her friend as Chrissie began to lick round Ivor's trembling tool. 'Room for one more,' asked Paula brightly and she bent her head down and sucked Ivor's tightening ballsack between her lips. Chrissie began to suck his cock in earnest, letting her tongue linger lovingly on his sensitive skin as it travelled the length of his pulsating shaft. When she felt he was about to explode, she started to swallow in anticipation of the rush of hot, sticky seed which seconds later shot out of his quivering cock. Paula released his balls from her mouth and joined Chrissie in licking up the drains of creamy jism that remained on Ivor's knob.

'You girls should have waited till they brought breakfast and we could have tried drinking tea like Woody, Tony Godfrey's American friend,' grinned Ivor. Chrissie pulled on his wet, semi-hard shaft and replied: 'I'll tell Mike Lewis all about the way you've fucked so many Glasgow girls, if we have any more sauce from you.'

'That won't matter so long as you don't tell him that Ivor supports Hibernian. That really would mean that he'd never get the job,' said Paula. But before Ivor could reply, a knock at the door signalled the arrival of breakfast.

Ivor pulled the sash around his dressing gown and Paula popped back between the sheets as he opened the door. 'Come on in,' said Ivor. As they wheeled two large trolleys into the room, the two waitresses gaped at the bed in which lay Paula, Beth, Tony and Brian.

'We're all close friends here,' said Ivor as he gave each of the girls a pound note. 'I'd be grateful if you'd make sure we're not disturbed.'

They thanked him for the generous tip and one of the girls suppressed a giggle as Brian Lipman's eyes fluttered open and he let out an audible fart before muttering: 'Morning all, who fancies a fuck?'

This reminded Ivor of something important and after he shepherded out the waitresses he hurried back and shook Brian by the shoulder. 'Come on Brian, for fuck's sake, wake up,' he hissed in the photographer's ear. 'You've missed your sodding 'plane. How the hell are you going to get the photographs processed in time for Julie to send them out this afternoon?'

Brian hauled himself and cleared his throat. 'Don't get your knickers in a twist, old son. I sent the films down to London last night by courier and young Warren's coming in at eight o'clock this morning to develop them. I'll catch the ten forty-five flight and I'll be in the studio in good time to check all is well. I've phoned Julie at Cable and arranged to meet her in your office at two o'clock. Okay?'

'Thanks Brian, well done,' said a much relieved Ivor. Brian smacked his lips and said: 'What's under the chafing dishes, Ivor? All that fucking has made me bloody hungry.'

He jumped out of bed and grunted: 'Go on, you three, don't let the food get cold. You start and I'll catch up after I've had a wee and a wash.'

'We'd better wake the other Sleeping Beauties,' advised Chrissie and she slid her hand underneath the sheet and tugged Tony Godfrey's shaft which woke the suave playboy up with a start. 'Ouch! What's happening here? Chrissie, let go my cock,' he cried out.

'Sorry, I just wanted to wake you up,' she apologised but at least Tony's cry had woken up Beth who was a very heavy sleeper. In a few minutes, they were all eating a hearty breakfast for, like Brian, the night's exertions had given them all a hearty appetite.

Half an hour later, Brian crunched the last piece of buttered toast between his teeth and in a slight misquotation from *Macbeth* enquired: 'Well folks, when shall we six meet again, in thunder, lightning or in rain?'

'When the hurly burly's done, when the battle's lost and won,' answered Beth promptly.

'That will be ere the set of sun,' continued Tony and Ivor grunted: 'Let's hope you're right, Beth. Wow, wouldn't it be grand to have a slap-up reunion party after Four Seasons tops the dog food sales in Scotland and Cable Publicity wins the Jetstream Showers account?'

Before anyone could reply there was a knock on the door. Brian hauled himself up and said: 'I'll go, it must be the waitresses who want to take away the trolleys.' But when he opened the door he let out a cry of surprise: 'Bloody hell, what are you doing here! Come on in, mate! Is Ivor expecting you?'

'Who is it?' Ivor called out. He scrambled to his feet as Brian brought Craig Grey into the bedroom. 'Oh, hiya

Craig! Good to see you! You're nice and early, I didn't expect you up here until tonight.'

'I decided to catch the seven o'clock flight from Heathrow,' said Cable Publicity's research director and the three girls looked with interest at the handsome, smartly-dressed new arrival. Craig Grey was a slim, good-looking young man in his mid-twenties, with long dark hair and a sun-tanned Mediterranean complexion that accentuated the attractive colour of his bluish-green eyes.

'Let me introduce you,' said Ivor but Brian clapped him on the shoulder and said: 'I'll be off, mate. I have to pack before catching that ten forty-five flight back home. 'Bye, everybody. Remember now, girls, you've got my card. Any time you're in London, don't forget to give me a call.'

'I must be going too,' said Beth, slipping on her coat. With a twinkle in her eye she made her farewells and then added: 'Thank you for having me, Ivor – and the rest of you!'

After Brian and Beth had left, Chrissie said: 'Don't take it personally, Craig, but Paula and I must also be on our way. I'll telephone Mike Lewis before we go. It's a bit early but I'll see if he's already at his desk.'

Whilst Chrissie waited for the hotel operator to connect her to her brother-in-law's office, Ivor asked Craig if he had a good flight up to Glasgow. 'Yes, I quite enjoyed it. The weather was good and the flight was so smooth that I almost fell asleep. In fact I would have done if there hadn't been a ripe slice of hanky panky between a young teenage couple in the seats on the other side of the gangway.'

Paula cocked her head and commented: 'Hanky-panky on a crowded 'plane at half past seven in the morning? They must have been a bit desperate.'

Craig returned her smile and said: 'I suppose they must

have been members of the Mile High Club – or if they weren't, perhaps they were applying for membership! But the plane was half-empty, and like me, this couple were lucky enough to be sitting by themselves in a row of three seats. We were at the very back of the plane and nobody was sitting in the rows directly in front of us.

'We were served breakfast almost immediately after take-off and I settled down to read the newspaper. At first, all was quiet but after a few minutes I could hear little squeaks and squeals and muffled giggling coming from the other side of the gangway. I looked across to see what was going on and boy, did I get a surprise! They had folded back the arm rests and the girl was lying down with her feet towards the window and the guy was straddled across her with his knees on either side of her body.

'He'd undone her blouse and taken off her bra and was rubbing his hands across her bare breasts whilst she was fumbling with the zip of his trousers. I could hardly believe my eyes when as bold as brass she pulled out his stiff prick and he started to tit-fuck her, sliding his shaft across her nipples and then in and out between the cleft of her breasts which she pushed together whilst he jerked his cock back and forth.

'I heard him gasp: "I'm coming!" and then, would you believe, she grabbed hold of his twitching cock and sucked it into her mouth. She bobbed her head to and fro for a few seconds and then he spunked into her mouth.'

Ivor took a deep breath. 'Bloody hell, if that doesn't take the biscuit!'

'And the pie, coffee and biscuits as well,' agreed Craig cheerfully. 'Well, she licked his prick clean and then he shoved his tool back into his pants and she buttoned up her blouse and they sat cuddled together for the rest of the flight.'

Paula had been listening closely to Craig's tale about the couple's reckless behaviour. She cleared her throat and said: 'Well, I could never make love in public like that, and frankly, I think it's out of order. I mean to say, fucking with friends is one thing but to screw in front of strangers is way over the top for my liking.'

Craig turned to her and flashed a wide smile at the pretty girl. 'My thoughts exactly, Paula,' he agreed. 'And I suppose my disapproval must have shown in my face, because about ten minutes later, whilst the girl was in the loo, the young chap came over to me and made fulsome apologies for their loss of control. And here's a coincidence, Ivor, this guy turned out to be none other than Ruff Trayde's young brother!'

'Ruff's young brother – surely you don't mean Clive?' exclaimed a surprised Ivor, for he had always believed the nineteen-year-old youth to be of similar sexual orientation to his pop star sibling.

'The very same,' said Craig with a vulpine grin. 'Oh, yes, I know that you all thought that he was a you-know-what but after what I saw with my own eyes, I promise you that either the gossip's untrue or he swings both ways.'

Ivor stroked his chin and said thoughtfully: 'Enter Rumour, painted full of tongues. Goes to show you how much mischief idle talk can do, doesn't it. Hold on a mo, though, Craig, didn't Clive join a PR agency in Birmingham after he left school?'

'Quite right, Ivor. Clive and I had a little chat after his apology and I happened to ask him if he travelled to Scotland frequently. And that's how I found out that he was an assistant account executive at a small consultancy called Leslie Jackey Associates in Solihull.'

'Never heard of them,' said Ivor promptly. 'But for

God's sake, you're not now going to tell me that this firm's after the Jetstream account!'

Craig Grey nodded. 'That I am, sor,' he replied in a thick if not very recognisable Irish accent which he quickly dropped as he added in more serious vein: 'Whilst I was talking to him, it suddenly occurred to me that he might be going after Jetstream's business, so I asked him point blank what brought him up to Bonnie Scotland. He made no secret of it. He said that his company was hoping to work for the fastest-growing bathroom fittings manufacturer in Britain. I can't believe that he wasn't talking about our mutual friends.

'Of course, when he asked me why I was flying up here I said that I was lecturing at a seminar in Edinburgh – which is true enough, isn't it? Mind, to throw him off the scent, when he asked what the seminar was about, I told him that I was a doctor specialising in sexual problems! That's when he mentioned his brother –'

'Yes, well that's another story,' said Ivor hastily, automatically closing down a conversation about Ruff Trayde's sexual activities whenever anyone from outside Cable Publicity was nearby. 'So we have competition then, though I'd like to know why Leslie Jackey Associates, whoever they are, are sending a boy to do a man's job.'

Chrissie had now finished her telephone conversation with her brother-in-law and she was able to answer this question. 'Mike's just been speaking to me about that company. It's because Harold Jackey's a cousin of the managing director's wife,' she explained. 'And so the guy thinks that the account is in the bag. He says that Clive Mumford isn't much more than a delivery boy who is coming with a girl from their art department to show off their publicity ideas.'

'A bit over-confident, I'd say,' suggested Tony Godfrey, joining in the conversation for the first time. 'Especially if Mr Jackey is only the wife's cousin. If I were Jetstream's managing director, I'd be more than a little miffed about only being offered the monkey rather than the organ grinder. On the other hand, if the Jetstream fellow's under his wife's thumb, I suppose it doesn't matter too much.'

'Mike didn't say anything about that,' said Chrissie. 'But if you would like to see him for a preliminary meeting, Ivor, he's free at three o'clock this afternoon. I hope I did the right thing, but I said you'd be there.'

Ivor leaned over and kissed her cheek. 'I should say so, love, thanks again for everything. Look, let's all meet up again tonight. Craig and I'll go to Edinburgh but it'll be no problem to rendezvous back here.'

'Paula and I have tomorrow off,' said Chrissie brightly. 'Why don't we meet you in Edinburgh? It's a beautiful city and you boys shouldn't leave Scotland without a trip round Old Reekie. Should they, Paula?'

'Edinburgh's super,' agreed her friend. 'Though I don't know it that well myself and I'd love to go round the town with you.'

'Okay with me,' said Ivor and Craig said: 'No problem for me either, I'm already booked in at the North British tomorrow night and I'm sure I can book us all in for tonight as well. Girls, you don't mind sharing a double room, do you?'

He looked at Tony Godfrey and said: 'Ivor hasn't introduced us but your face looks very familiar. I'm Craig Grey, head of research at Cable Publicity. No, don't tell me your name, I'm sure I know it.'

They shook hands and then Craig snapped his fingers. 'Got it! You're Tony Godfrey, aren't you? I saw you on the box a couple of weeks ago being interviewed by Donald Farmer. What was the programme now? Oh yes, *The Idle Rich.* I thought he gave you a hard time.'

'Not really, I don't work in the usual sense of the word and I do have more money than I need,' said Tony with a modest shrug. 'And he was kind enough to say that he thought I was an exception to the usual maxim adopted by the very wealthy, that when it comes to money, enough is never enough.

'But look here, you don't need me around to be the spare prick at the wedding. I was planning to go back to London this afternoon anyway.'

'Oh no, you mustn't go,' cried Paula. 'You're a lovely man and you have a wonderful cock. You must come to Edinburgh with us!'

'Of course you must,' Craig chimed in warmly. 'I didn't finish telling you what happened on my flight. When Clive went to wash his hands I chatted up the girl friend and she gave me her card. Clive's going to meet some old family friends tonight and Sophie wasn't invited to go with him. So I asked her out to dinner this evening. Therefore we do need you to make up the numbers, Tony, besides the fact that I've read so much about you, I'm dying to ask you some questions that they *didn't* put to you on that television programme!'

'Well, so long as I won't be in the way,' said Tony, who was only too pleased to let himself be persuaded to stay. Despite his playboy image, he did not in fact lead the kind of riotous lifestyle which the gossip columnists sketched for him, and he had no pressing engagements back in London. 'I know Edinburgh quite well and as you say, Chrissie, Edinburgh's a super place in summer. I came up for the Festival last year and had a great time there.'

'I'll bet you did,' said Paula, snuggling up to him. 'What

was her name? Come on, we've just time to hear all about it before we grab a taxi.'

Tony blushed and said: 'It was rather special, I suppose. Now Chrissie and Paula may know what it's like to be in Edinburgh during the Festival. The city's packed with tourists and you rush about going from one thing to another. Well, I'd just been to a matinee at the Assembly Rooms in George Street and the weather was so nice that I bought myself an ice-cream and walked down to Princes Street and into the gardens below the Castle. I sat on a bench and was idly watching the people go by whilst I licked my ice-cream. I'd just finished crunching my wafer when I noticed two extremely pretty blonde girls dressed in identical white mini-dresses walking towards the bench. One was supporting the other who was hobbling badly and when I walked towards them to offer my help, I could see that they were extremely pretty identical twins.

'I guessed that they were foreign from the cut of their clothes – it's funny how you can always tell – and I was proved right when the injured girl said in a slightly lilting Scandinavian accent. "Thank you very much. I twisted my foot as we came down the steps from the Castle. I'm sure I will be alright after I have rested it."

'Now as the holder of a Scouts First Aid badge, I could genuinely put my skills to good use! "I hope so," I said, squatting down on my haunches in front of her. "May I examine your ankle? I'm not a doctor but I probably know enough to check that you haven't broken a bone."

'I lifted her foot gently into my hands and I trembled when I looked up because her thighs were slightly apart. Her mini-skirt was so tiny that I could see right up to her crotch which was covered by the tiniest little pair of panties which barely covered her bush! I breathed hard and concentrated on examining her ankle. Fortunately it was only twisted and she was soon on the road to recovery.

'Anyway, we began chatting and we introduced ourselves. The girls were indeed twins and hailed from a little Swedish town called Nykopping, just south of Stockholm although at the time they were both in their first year at the University of Uppsala. I was staying in a suite at the Caledonian which was only a few minutes walk away, and I invited Brigitte and Gail to have tea with me at the hotel.

'We had a marvellous tea at the Cally and we got on together really well. Like all Swedes the girls spoke perfect English and like me they were great theatregoers although, being students, they couldn't afford to go to the higher-priced performances. They also told me that they loved opera and wanted to hear that new Israeli tenor, David Tzanerofski, sing *Turandot* that evening. But, they said, the cheaper seats had been sold out many weeks beforehand.

'"Don't worry, I'll get us tickets," I said and I went across to the porter's desk to book them. Unfortunately, the performance was a sell-out and the girls' faces fell when I returned to tell them the news. "Wait on though," I said. "Come up to my suite and I'll make a couple of telephone calls. There are other ways to get tickets."

'Upstairs, I sat the girls down on the settee and poured them large vodka and orange juices whilst I called an old friend of mine, John Gibson of the *Edinburgh Evening News*. He knows everyone who's anyone in town. He gave me the telephone number of a girl he knew who was in the chorus and, to cut a long story short, for the promise of two five pound notes in a brown envelope to be handed in at the stage door before curtain-up, I managed to obtain three house seats in the middle stalls.

'"It is very kind of you, Tony, but we cannot afford such expensive seats," said Gail, who was the twin who had hurt her foot. "And we cannot accept more hospitality from you."

'"Nonsense," I said, squeezing her hand between mine. "I can well afford it and all I ask in exchange is that you both come back here for supper after the performance. Now, where are you staying? I'll arrange for a private car to pick us up and take us back from the theatre as we might have a problem finding a taxi."

'I didn't have to do much more persuading. The opera was terrific – Tzanerofski took eight curtain calls – and the girls looked magnificent in low-cut evening dresses. Some press photographer took a shot of us going into the theatre and it appeared next day in *The Scotsman*! Anyhow, I had arranged a buffet supper in my suite and the smoked salmon platters and champagne kept the adrenalin flowing. Brigitte switched on the radio and asked me if I wanted to dance. My luck was in because just as I took her in my arms, the music changed to something slow and romantic and when she threw her arms around my neck and moulded her soft curves against my throbbing erection, I knew that the evening would end on an even higher note than Tzanerofski was capable of singing!

'But then Gail joined in and made it a threesome. We smooched around the room with our bodies pressed tightly against one another. I should add that we were all slightly tipsy and when we collapsed in a heap on the settee, we were shrieking with laughter. "Sshh, we'll disturb the other guests," I warned the girls as I cuddled them both tightly against me, for I was the meat in the sandwich, so to speak. Then Gail said something in Swedish to her sister and that's when the fun and games really started. Brigitte took hold of my hand and placing it across her breasts, she let her hand travel down to my groin and felt the huge bulge in my lap.

'"Would you like to fuck us, Tony?" she enquired and I was so taken aback that I could hardly answer her. "Yes please," I gulped and Gail said: "Well, wait here five minutes and then come into the bedroom."

'I did as I was told and my heart jumped when I entered the bedroom. There were the two girls lying naked on the bed waiting for me. They were both absolutely gorgeous, tall and lithe with small but beautifully rounded breasts and long, long legs which seemed to go up to their armpits. "Come on, Tony, don't just stand there," ordered Brigitte and I quickly undressed and took my place between them.

'Gail grabbed hold of my prick whilst Brigitte kissed me and sucked my tongue inside her mouth. My eyes were closed as I caressed Brigitte's breasts but I could feel Gail sliding down the bed and I could feel her licking my body all over till she came to my prick. Once there, she slipped my cock between her lips and started to suck me off whilst Brigitte broke off our kiss to straddle herself over me so that her silky blonde bush was directly above my face. She lowered her furry curls onto my mouth and I began to tongue her juicy cunt, licking along the sides of her slit and then inserting the tip of my tongue between her love lips which made her gasp with pleasure. At the same time, Gail gobbled in almost all of my shaft between her lips and washed my knob with her tongue so sensuously that I couldn't hold back for more than about thirty seconds. When she felt me coming, she squeezed my balls and I shot my load down her throat.

'Then my tonguing brought Brigitte off and she pressed her pussy hard down on my mouth, grinding her cunny from side to side as the love juice spurted out of her crack and dribbled over my nose and lips. I brought up my hands and played with her clitty and Gail tweaked her titties which sent her wild with delight and she came again and again all over my face.

'The girls took up new positions and I fucked Brigitte's sopping cunt doggie-style whilst Gail licked my balls. Later, after I had recovered, Brigitte sucked me off whilst I finger-fucked her sister. We frolicked on till almost five in the morning when the girls crept out of the suite down to the hall where the chauffeur was patiently waiting to drive them back to their digs.

'We had another session the next evening but then I had to fly back to London for a charity concert I had arranged months ago. Alas, I haven't seen the girls since, but we do keep in touch through the occasional letter, and they always write that if I ever go to Uppsala, we must take things up again from where we left off. I can't say that I haven't been tempted to take a long weekend out there, but hopefully the twins will be coming to London for a holiday in the autumn. As you can imagine, I can hardly wait to see them again!

'Anyhow, that's the story, folks, and I'm sure that in such attractive company, I'll enjoy myself just as much on this trip as I did during my last stay in Edinburgh!' he ended gallantly.

Paula kissed his ear and with a little giggle, said softly: 'We'll have to make sure that you do, Tony Godfrey, but you really are a very naughty boy. Your sexy story has made my knickers so damp that I should really take them off before we go.'

'There's no time for that,' said Chrissie, pulling her friend away from Tony's side. 'We can't even stop for a quick knee-trembler or we'll be late for work. Ivor, before we leave, quickly run through the arrangements for the rest of the day.'

'Well, I've a taxi waiting outside to take you both home and then on to the supermarket. Just sign the cabbie's bill, by the way, and it'll go on my account, no problem. About tonight though, would it be possible for you girls to meet us in Edinburgh? That would save a lot of hassle *schlapping* back and forth after Craig and I have seen Mike Lewis.'

'Sure, why not?' said Paula. 'Why don't we meet you at around eight o'clock at the hotel, it's directly above Waverley Station. If you aren't able to book us in there, we can go on to wherever you have managed to find rooms for us.'

'Good, I'll have the hotel send over two rail tickets to Edinburgh in an envelope to you at Websters this afternoon.'

After hugs and kisses all round, the girls departed and Tony followed shortly afterwards to go back to his hotel and pack his case. 'I'll meet you at one o'clock sharp at Queen Street Station,' he called out as he left. After Ivor had packed his bag and arranged for the equipment he had brought for the Four Seasons launch to be sent back to London, Craig called the North British Hotel and, to his relief, found there was no problem in booking the extra accommodation needed.

They met Tony at Queen Street Station in good time to catch the one-fifteen train to Edinburgh. Once settled down in their comfortable first-class seats, the three men dozed through most of the forty-five minute journey to Scotland's capital city.

As Paula had said, the hotel was situated literally above Waverley Station and a lift whizzed them up from the platform to the reception desk. 'This was built as a railway hotel sixty years ago,' remarked Tony Godfrey. 'Even the big clock on the tower was set five minutes fast so that passengers would have time to catch their trains.'

They checked in and unpacked but Ivor and Craig had no time to accept Tony Godfrey's invitation to enjoy a cool beer and a sandwich in the hotel bar before leaving for their appointment with Mike Lewis at Jetstream's headquarters out near Edinburgh Airport.

'We'll see you when we get back,' said Ivor as he asked a passing porter to order a taxi. 'I reckon we'll be back around five o'clock.'

'I'll have the kettle on,' said Tony and he wished them good luck as they walked to the door. In the taxi, Ivor and Craig scanned the latest information about bathroom fittings which the head of Cable Publicity's research department had brought with him up from London.

'How much of our hand do we show?' asked Craig, as Ivor paid off the taxi outside Jetstream's gates.

'Not too much,' Ivor advised as they walked through to the front of the company's office block. 'I'd rather do more listening than talking at this stage and save the facts and figures for the managing director.'

Inside the reception area, Ivor flashed a friendly smile to the dour-looking middle-aged woman on the switchboard. 'Good afternoon, my name's Belling and my colleague and I have an appointment with Mr Lewis.'

'Oh yes, he's expecting you,' said the telephonist, after checking through her notebook. 'Mr Lewis called in a while ago to say that he's sorry but he might be a little late. But you're welcome to sit in his office and wait for him there. He shouldn't be much more than ten minutes or so. Go through that door, turn right and Mr Lewis's office is the third door on the left hand side.'

'Thank you, I'm sure we'll find it,' said Ivor politely but

as they walked through and turned right as instructed, he muttered to Craig: 'That's not the way I'd look after people. I'd never let strangers waltz in like that. After all, we could be important clients who should be cossetted and cherished, or we could be villains doing a spot of industrial espionage on behalf of a competitor, or plain old-fashioned burglars out to knock off a couple of electric typewriters.'

'H'mm, good thinking Carruthers,' said Craig as they reached Mike Lewis's office. Ivor flung open the door – only to jump back to collide against his colleague at the sound of a startled scream from inside the room.

It was hard to know who was more surprised, Ivor and Craig or the shapely auburn-haired girl who had positioned herself at the side of the large wooden desk. Her feet were firmly planted on the floor although she was leaning forward over the desk with her skirt pulled up over her waist and her panties lying down by her ankles. Behind her stood a tall, slim young man whose trousers and underpants covered his shoes and who was slewing his cock in and out of the crevice of her ample buttocks. His face was screwed up as he approached his climax, oblivious of Ivor and Craig's presence at the door. He had evidently judged his partner's anguished shriek to be one of ecstasy as opposed to one of astonishment, for he jerked his hips faster and faster until, with a hoarse grunt, he withdrew his twitching cock and spurted his spunk all over the girl's rounded bum cheeks.

'A-a-a-g-h! A-a-a-g-h! Marie, my wee lass, that was the best ever,' he groaned and then, following the direction of the girl's frenzied pointing, he jumped back away from her, his cock still dribbling out the last drains of seed from his ejaculation.

'Oh my God! Who the fuck are you?' he shouted. His face turned white as he frantically tried to pull up his pants and trousers. Marie slid down from the desk and adjusted her dress before diving down to pull up her panties.

'Mike Lewis? I'm Ivor Belling and this is my colleague, Craig Grey, Cable Publicity's head of research,' said Ivor smoothly, though his mind was already working out the pluses and minuses of catching the prospective client *in flagrente delicto*. On one hand, Mike Lewis would be grateful for his silence, though on the other he might well wish never to see anyone from Cable Publicity within a hundred miles radius of his office. However, he would know that Ivor was a friend of his sister-in-law Chrissie. This might well lead him to ensure that she never found out about this escapade by keeping Ivor in his corner through doing his best to get Cable Publicity appointed as Jetstream's public relations consultants.

However, as it turned out, Ivor's speculations were made unnecessary when the young man croaked: 'I'm not Mike Lewis. He's out at a meeting and isn't expected back till three fifteen.'

'Ah, then in that case, we'll wait here for him as your receptionist suggested,' said Craig, pulling up a chair whilst the erstwhile Romeo fled and the pretty auburn-haired girl smoothed down her miniskirt and said: 'I'm Marie, Mike's secretary. I'm dreadfully sorry about –'

'Nothing to be sorry about, we came, we saw, we enjoyed and now the whole incident's been completely erased from our memory banks, hasn't it, Ivor?' said Craig cheerfully.

'Absolutely, so when might we expect to see Mike?' asked Ivor. The girl looked at her watch. 'Drat! My watch has stopped at half past two, which is why I didn't tell Jock to sling his hook when he started getting fruity just now. We are engaged, by the way, so please forgive us.'

'As Craig just told you, nothing untoward happened whilst we waited for Mike,' said Ivor and he added with a grin: 'And if you could rustle up a cup of tea, I'll give you a written guarantee to that effect!'

She looked at him with a grateful expression. 'Thanks, Mr Belling, I'll put the kettle on right now and see if I can find some choccie biscuits too. What's the time? Five past three? Mike shouldn't be much more than five minutes.'

In fact there was only time for Ivor and Craig to settle themselves into their chairs and take out notepads and pens before Mike Lewis breezed into his office. 'Hello there, I'm so sorry to have kept you waiting. Now one of you gentlemen must be Ivor Belling. Good to meet you! Chrissie has told me all about you and a friend of mine who works at J Walter Thompson said some very complimentary things about your agency when I called him this morning.'

Oh-ho, here's a professional, thought Ivor, as he returned Mike Lewis's greeting and introduced Craig Grey. He carefully studied Mike Lewis whilst Craig sketched out some details about Cable Publicity and the prospective client asked a couple of shrewd questions. Ivor was impressed by the burly, handsome man in his late twenties, a Lowland Scot from Ayrshire who spoke with a cool, clear enunciation which gave him an aura of competence and trust.

'We need to bang the drum about our products,' said Jetstream's rising star. 'And we need to be pretty bloody quick about it or we won't even keep our share of the market let alone climb up and slug it out with the leaders.

We can't afford a huge advertising spend so we need a smart, hot-shot PR agency to help us spread the word. Can you help us, Ivor?'

Ivor drew up his chair. 'Yes,' he said. 'I think we can.'

TO BE CONTINUED